Morning MilkingFarm

C.M. NASCOSTA
a Monster Bait Romance

C.M. NASCOSTA

Morning Glory Milking Farm

MEDUÂS
EDITORIALE

Dedicated to all of my Milking Assistants — your support means the world

&

A lightning storm of love to Irym & her family for indulging my "make it frothier"
fantasies at the expense of their kitchen
— all the aloha

&

Exceptional gratitude to Ella Flynn for her eagle eyes and boundless enthusiasm

For everyone wishing the Hallmark Channel would do us a solid with an
Inhuman Lovers series — this series is for you
(Hallmark Channel — call me! I've got a great script!)

Contents

I   Part One

Chapter 1   3
Chapter 2   14
Chapter 3   24

II   Part Two

Chapter 4   39
Chapter 5   51
Chapter 6   63

III   Part Three

Chapter 7   73
Chapter 8   80
Chapter 9   88

IV   Part Four

Chapter 10   95
Chapter 11   104
Chapter 12   114

V   Part Five

Chapter 13   121
Chapter 14   135
Chapter 15   146

VI   HEA

Chapter 16   161
Chapter 17   176

About the Author   187
Also by C.M. Nascosta   188

I

Part One

Chapter 1

"T he goal for every client is a plentiful, speedy collection. That is the expectation with which you will approach every shift—getting our clients in and out and on with their day, all while maintaining our quality protocols. A plentiful, speedy collection makes for happy clients and a productive farm!"

The fox-like woman's beaming, sharp-edged smile froze, her glinting canines transformed into something sinister and vaguely threatening as Violet tapped the laptop, pausing the video for the third time that morning. She'd not yet made it past the introduction today, needing to repeatedly remind herself to breathe and stay upright and that she was home, so bolting out into the hallway and making a break for the elevator would make little sense, particularly if she wanted to avoid the uncomfortable scenario of her elderly neighbors hearing the sound of the video coming from her apartment and discovering what she was watching.

She thought of little old Mrs. Muehlstein from down the hall, a withered, hunched crone with the beginnings of dementia, accidentally wandering into the wrong apartment, catching sight of the instructional video, and having a stroke right there in the middle of the living room. *Is that what you want? For the last thing that sweet old woman sees is some minotaur getting a tug job? Get a fucking grip and make up your mind!*

Her portal access was only good for another eight hours; eight hours in which to decide whether or not she'd be a good fit for the team at Morning Glory Farm; if her jangling nerves and ever-present anxiety would allow her to take the plunge and click accept. The implication of her words and what exactly she'd be *gripping* if she took the job occurred to her then, and she moaned in mortification. It wasn't the first preposterous mental image she'd concocted since leaving Cambric Creek the previous afternoon, and Violet was certain, as she clicked play once more, that it wouldn't be the last.

* * *

4

The job listing had seemed too good to be true.

Now Hiring! Technicians and assistants, no prior experience required. On-the-job training, full benefits, flexible scheduling! Visit our web page for more information and apply today! (Morning Glory Farm is a subsidiary of Pfizzle Pharmaceuticals)

Violet had known it the moment it pinged on the hiring app, squinting at her phone screen in disbelief as she scrolled, nearly a week ago. No experience necessary, on-the-job training provided. Two weeks vacation and full benefits, including dental. *Dental!* She had no idea what a *milking technician* was nor what it entailed, but the advertised starting salary was higher than any belonging to the handful of jobs open in her degree field, none of which paid enough to comfortably keep a roof over her head.

The family upstairs had chosen that moment to begin what sounded like a good old-fashioned, barn-stomping square dance, reminding her that the roof over her head wasn't exactly anything to brag about, which made the fact that she struggled to pay her rent even more galling.

"Pumpkin, daddy and I have been talking . . . now, I know you're going to say no, but please just think about it, okay? We think you ought to consider coming home while you're looking for work." She'd practically been able to hear her mother raising a hand to hold off any protestations, could imagine it easily. "If you think you'd feel too crowded in the house now that Aunt Gracie is with us, we can clean out the loft over the garage. It would be like having your own little apartment! You wouldn't need to worry about rent, and you'd be out of that awful city . . . just promise me you'll think about it, alright? It doesn't make any sense to be wasting so much money before you've found something stable, and it would be so nice having you home."

She'd gripped the phone with whitened knuckles, trying to hold back her tears until disconnecting. Her mother always seemed to know when to call, always knew when she was at her lowest and most vulnerable—always with an abundance of love, overflowing with compassion and eager to help—but always at the *worst* fucking times. Moving to Bridgeton for grad school had always been a point of contention with her mother: too dangerous, too

5

expensive, too dirty, too far away. She hadn't wanted her only child moving to the big city, several hours away from her hugs and home-cooked meals and her own untreated anxiety disorder, but Violet had been adamant.

It was a bitter pill to swallow now, being forced to admit her mother was not wrong in her assessment. There was a particular sort of indignity that came along with being simultaneously well-educated and in dire straits financially. She had done everything right: had studied hard, made the Dean's list, participated in campus events, graduating with honors. But then by the time she'd earned her bachelor's degree, her chosen job field required a master's, sending her back to the classroom, taking out several loans to do so, confident that she'd begin her career immediately after graduation. Her part-time job in the urban development office actually put her degree to use, but they'd been upfront that it was unlikely to turn into a permanent position, not with the scads of people who had priority ahead of her. Bridgeton *was* too expensive, and Violet had come to admit that she didn't actually love living in the middle of a big, urban city the way she thought she would. Admitted it to herself, at least.

"If I don't find something soon I'm not going to have much of a choice," she'd agreed bitterly, pressing her tongue into the roof of her mouth as her mother cooed sympathetically. *Don't cry. If you start crying, she'll drive here tonight.*

In hindsight, putting herself into debt to work in the non-profit sector seemed almost comical; would have been a fucking riot, were it anyone else. Unfortunately, it was hard to appreciate the humor of the situation when she herself was the butt of the joke. There had been no crystal ball to show her that the job market would bottom out, no sidewalk soothsayer to warn her away from the debt she was taking on. The near future had no clarion call, and so she'd never suspected she'd find herself overqualified for seventy-five percent of the jobs with openings and unable to pay back her student loans with the entry-level salaries they offered.

She was tired of struggling to pay her rent; was certain she was giving herself an ulcer stressing over her inability to repay her loans and remitting the bare minimum on her nearly maxed-out credit cards, but the thought of moving home, back to the boring little town she'd lived in her entire life, where no one ever left and no one ever did anything but have more kids to ensure future generations of drudgery, to the loft above her parent's garage, currently filled with boxes from Aunt Gracie's house and evidence of her mother's hobbies pursued and long since abandoned, was not one she could abide.

Now here was this job, a potential lifeline if she got it. She'd clicked the "apply now" button without another moment of hesitation. *Anything would be better than moving home. Who cares what it's for.*

Famous last words, she'd been forced to admit the previous day, squirming in her seat as the training video had been queued up, glancing surreptitiously at the other prospective new hires in attendance. A green-skinned woman with broad shoulders and curving tusks, whose long, black braid sat heavily on her shoulder; a slender troll who'd scarcely looked up from her phone since they'd entered the video room; an anxious-seeming young man with long, rabbit-like ears who carried a water bottle emblazoned with the local university's logo; and a pair of goblins who seemed to know each other, if their non-stop chatter was any indication. There was not another human in sight, but Violet had been half-expecting that.

The interview process had been simple and straightforward: an online portal to apply, followed by a video call, during which she'd been asked about her work history and organizational skills. She'd been invited to visit the facility for the "final step in the process," traveling to Cambric Creek, a neighboring suburb that boasted a multi-species population—a longer commute than she'd been hoping for, but as the GPS led her through the suburb's quaint downtown, past shops and restaurants until housing developments gave way to agriculture and industrial parkways, she reminded herself of the full benefits offered. Before she knew it, she was turning into a long, circular driveway, parking in front of a building with the outer facade of a great red barn, praying this might be the break she needed.

It's going to be fine. You can do this, who cares if you're the only human. You really need this job.

The aesthetic design of the building went out of its way to invoke the friendly feeling of a neighborhood farmstead, both inside and out. Artificial turf in the lobby with the ceiling painted to look like a summer sky; bright, punchy colors that invoked gleaming tractors and richly-painted barns, with milk glass vases of daisies on every surface. They had spared no expense creating the visuals, Violet thought as she'd filled out tax forms and on boarding paperwork before joining the small cluster of other prospective hires. The farmhouse aesthetic ended within the sterile white hallways of the employee corridors, the synthetic turf flooring of the lobby giving way to smooth linoleum and the bright colors smoothing out to cool eggshell and ice blue. A strange prickle of apprehension had prickled up her neck, a shiver she'd attributed to jitters and the strangeness of being the only human in the group.

"Welcome to Morning Glory! We appreciate you all taking time out of your days to visit the farm!" The tiefling standing before them had cool blue skin and the curling horns of a ram, and her smile was overly wide. "Today we'll be giving you a tour of the facility, as well as the opportunity to register on our online portal and watch some process videos. Your portal access is good for twenty-four hours, in which time you'll need to decide whether you'll be a good fit for our team. If the answer is yes, you can input your schedule availability, and you'll be put into the rotation for the following week." The girl had paused to smile brightly once more, a spade-tipped tail swishing behind her. "Your first two weeks on the job will be shadowing technicians who have been with us from the beginning, so rest assured—you'll be shown everything you need to learn before you'll be on your own!"

She trailed on the edge of the group for the next hour, feeling awkward and out-of-place as they followed the tiefling in and out of various rooms, but she hadn't been any closer to understanding what exactly the job she'd applied for entailed by the time they were led to a large classroom-like space, taking seats at the tables as the first training video was queued up. The overhead lights had dimmed and instantly the chatter in the room had ceased, everyone straightening to attention as the video began. A bright-eyed woman with the features of a fox had filled the screen, beaming from the center of the same lobby the prospective employees had gathered in that morning, wearing a black and white Holstein-printed apron over a white, cap-sleeve top. Behind her, filling the upholstered lobby chairs, was a cluster of minotaurs.

"Welcome to Morning Glory Farm! Incorporated nearly a decade ago, our mission has remained the same since the day our lab processed its first specimen—to uphold the integrity of the genetic material in our care, to set a new standard in pharmaceutical processing that the entire industry would model, and to provide a client-first attitude in all we do. Our brand new, state-of-the-art facility in Cambric Creek marries all three tenets, putting the client experience at the center of our collection process. As a milking technician on our collection floor, you will be tasked with ensuring a plentiful, speedy collection, processed in accordance with our standards in safety and sterility. You've already taken a tour of the facility, now you'll get to see our process in action . . . follow me!"

On the screen, the fox-woman had twinkled as one of the minotaurs behind her rose, following her through a set of double doors. Violet had felt a sudden wave of nerves grip her, an inexplicable panic that had tightened her throat and made her grip the sides of her chair as if she needed to hold on for dear life. *A plentiful, speedy collection . . . what does that mean? What do the minotaurs have to do with anything?* She'd had no idea why, no clue what caused the sudden premonition to squeeze her heart, but a tiny, panicked voice in her head had begun to whisper *run!*

"As you've already seen, our state-of-the-art collection rooms have been designed for both client comfort and ease of execution by our milking technicians. The bi-level design puts the tools you need right at your fingertips, keeping the process seamless and efficient. A dedicated team ensures each collection room is fully stocked and set up for every client so there is no lag time, setting you up for success."

On the screen, several feet above the cheerful woman on the upper portion of the curiously designed room, the minotaur lowered his pants. Violet wasn't sure if her strangled gasp had been swallowed up by the room, for no one had turned or shushed her, and she'd been very nearly able to convince herself she'd imagined seeing the quick glance of a rounded backside and swishing tail as the camera panned over a chrome appliance in the center of the room where the smiling woman stood . . . but there could be no question a moment later when a semi-erect minotaur penis appeared through an opening beside the woman's head. Heavy-looking testicles hung behind the jutting appendage, and the fox-woman beamed, depressing the pump of a large bottle on the table beside her, coating her gloved hands in oil.

"Once your room is set up and your client arrives, you'll need to ensure the collection unit is loaded and your client clipboard in order. Then there's only one thing left to do—" her smile widened, showing a row of blinding-white teeth, offset with long, sharp, completely inhuman canines, and her hands raised, gripping the erection without a moment of hesitation—"start milking."

* * *

That human men placed an enormous importance on their dicks was no surprise to her. The whole world seemed to be designed for cocks, after all. Offices that were too cold, seat belts that cut across the neck instead of sitting comfortably across the chest, medicines that had only ever been tested on one segment of the population. Modern conveniences had been designed with only one half of the population in mind, at least in the human world, so the discovery that there was an entire underground industry devoted to human men's erections was not at all surprising. Learning the lengths to which pharmaceutical companies were willing to go to ensure the production of those erection-enhancing little blue pills didn't slow, however, was eye-opening.

Bull semen, specifically Minotaur semen, was a major component in giving the pills the *oomph* their devotees needed . . . and she, in her new role, if she decided to take the job, would be responsible for collecting it.

She needed to decide by that evening, a decision that seemed as daunting as it had in the hours after she'd left the farm in a daze as it did now. She'd spent the rest of the previous evening slumped over her laptop, watching slack-jawed as the beaming fox-woman in the video jerked off minotaur after minotaur; huge, hulking bullmen resting comfortably against the padded breeding stocks, their thick members prominently displayed for the technician who stood a level below them. Her dreams that night had been a twisted tangle of sharp-smiling teeth and the silhouette of huge men, the shadows of their horns completely engulfing her as she was pushed to stand beneath them until she'd woken gasping in a sweaty tangle, unsure of where she was or what she was contemplating.

Now that she'd watched the video repeatedly, small details she might have overlooked otherwise jumped out at her: the minotaur's girthy members vaguely resembled their human counterparts, but there was no comparing the *size*. Commensurate with the heft of the hulking bullmen, their cocks were long and impossibly thick, riddled in veins with prominent, dome-like heads. Some bore the same coloration of their owner's varied hides, while others were bubblegum pink or deep red, flushed with the blood that engorged them. She wondered, watching as the technician moved her oiled hands in a continuous twist down the rigid shaft, if the men in the video had been specifically chosen as displays of the finest minotaur meat available, and considered that reality might not match up with the glossy media, the same as it rarely did with human men.

"It's up to you to decide when the use of mechanical stimulation is necessary," the chipper woman said seriously into the camera. The implication was clear: if the men were taking too long, apply the cylinders of the milking machine to speed things along. Despite the fact she knew exactly what was coming, Violet began to breathe hard when the technician released her hands, letting the oiled cock bob as she took up one of the silver nozzles. The hum of the machine's air compressor was a steady white noise in the video, the mechanical arms within already pistoning, creating the rhythmic suction the minotaur was about to experience. Sure enough, the big bull grunted and jerked as the cylinder was eased down his straining cock, lowing deeply as the machine did its work.

"I like to continue providing manual stimulation at this point," the technician advised, and Violet whimpered, the same reaction she'd had each time she'd replayed this section numerous times the night before, when the woman

11

on the video began to rub at the huge, swollen testicles, pulling and squeezing as the minotaur bucked against the table. "Remember—the aim is a plentiful, speedy collection!"

A green light flicked to life on the machine, indicating the collection had commenced as the minotaur lowed again, his generous hips shaking the stocks above the chipper technician's head as he slammed against them. Violet's eyes didn't know where to dart on the screen: the rutting hips of the bullman, the cylinder sucking on the massive cock that jutted from the opening in the bench, or the twee, old-fashioned milk bottle at the base of the collection unit that was steadily being filled with white. In the end, she had dragged the video's progress indicator back repeatedly, the dozenth time she'd done so, giving each point of interest her absolute focus. The bottle was nearly full when the minotaur finally sagged in satisfaction, completely spent, and Violet did the same at her desk chair. *This is insane,* she told herself. *You can't do something like this, it's completely . . . lewd and vulgar and inappropriate! Just get a job at the coffee place on the corner.*

Is it though? A traitorous little voice piped up as she opened the small pantry cabinet, seeking something for breakfast. *It's a pharmaceutical company, a major multinational. It's not like you're working in some random guy's basement.* She wasn't sure what she'd expected to find in the cupboard, knowing full well she hadn't gone shopping in over a week. *It's not like you'd have to do it forever,* the voice continued as she walked up the sidewalk a short while later, heading to the discount grocery store several blocks away. *Just until you can get on your feet and pay down some bills; until you can find something in your field that actually pays a living wage.* She didn't know how long that would take, didn't know if there would ever be jobs in her field that paid more than a pittance . . .

The smell of the chain coffee shop on the corner caught her nose then, a waft of dark beans and sugary pastries, and Violet stopped in her tracks, heedless of the couple behind her, who was obliged to step into the street to move around her frozen form. *What the hell are you doing? You're almost twenty-six years old, and you can barely pay your rent. You're on your way to buy day-old bread and generic orange juice. Really, you're going to get a second job at this coffee shop? You'll need to because at this rate that's the only way you'll ever be able to afford to have anything there. This job could be a lifeline, remember? Stop being so stupid!*

She imagined the curl of the overpriced coffee leading her by the nose like an old-fashioned cartoon character as she crossed the street, pausing for only a moment before the shop's heavy doors. She was down to the last crumpled twenty-dollar bill at the bottom of her shoulder bag, and she actually *did* need to buy that no-brand orange juice, but she wanted breakfast, a proper breakfast. The coffee was burnt and bitter-tasting, doctored with overly-sweet syrups, and it and the honey-glazed challah braid had cost nearly half of that crumpled twenty, but it didn't matter, she thought, back in her apartment and in front of her laptop once more. Violet paused, closing her eyes as she bit into the still-warm bread, honey sticky on her lips, before clicking on the link that would take her to the schedule input screen. *Welcome to Morning Glory Farm!* It was going to be okay, she breathed. *You'll be on the schedule next week, and pretty soon you can drink all the over-priced burnt coffee you want.*

She queued up the video one last time before bed that night, after she'd received the confirmation email welcoming her to the farm and outlining what she'd be doing the following week. *Hands-on training will be provided.*

She was going to be good at this, Violet decided, dragging the cursor back to zoom in on the technician's hands, memorizing the way she gripped the slippery cock, the way her hands twisted. She'd always applied herself, given schoolwork and her part-time jobs her all, and this would be no exception. When the green light clicked on, she noted the way the minotaur's hips bucked against the breeding bench, his movement matching the rhythmic spatters against the inside of the bottle. His deep bellow of pleasure seemed to rattle in her brain as she settled in her bed, wondering if they would all make the same sort of noises; if they'd all buck and thrust wildly when they came, as the minotaurs in the video had.

Hands-on training, starting next week. You'll be finding out soon, she thought, ignoring the tingle between her thighs as she turned out the light.

Chapter 2

The collection floor needed to be clinically clean.

That was the first step covered in training, before even entering the room. Violet underlined the heading in her training binder, adding stars to either side of the bold-faced lettering, in an effort to emphasize the importance in her mind. *Collection Floor. Clinically Clean.*

"You just want to follow the steps, it's really that simple. Keep the workspace clean, it makes it easier for the next tech and keeps the day moving. You don't want to fall behind because someone else didn't call for a clean-up, because once you're behind you'll be behind all afternoon. Don't be the tech who throws off someone's whole day."

She had arrived that morning with a twist in her guts and what felt like sand coating her tongue, the same sort of nausea-inducing anxiety she'd always suffered from with every new class, new club, new experience. The pressure of being a perfectionist, the unarticulated terror of not being an automatic expert . . . it would pass, she knew, but that never calmed her jangling nerves or settled her stomach at the time.

When she'd made the drive to Cambric Creek the morning of her first visit to the farm, she'd been too focused on following the unfamiliar directions, turning when the smooth-accented AI said to turn. Now that the route was a bit more familiar, she'd found herself gazing out the window as she navigated her way through the picturesque town square with its gazebo and waterfall and expansive, green park. Shops and restaurants lined Main Street: bistros and boutiques, an occultist beside a shop with brightly colored stained glass windows, an interesting-looking bookshop and a nail salon boasting a promotion on "talon dips." The rich scent of coffee teased at her nose when she stopped at a light, coming from a wide-windowed storefront with black awnings and curling white lettering, and her stomach growled. Violet had a feeling it would be of a higher quality brew than the seventy-eight-cent gas station latte in her cup holder, a daily indulgence that she poured into a floral tumbler so that she appeared to be sipping one of the craft beverages from the chain near her apartment. *Better quality and probably a whole lot more expensive.*

A family of mothpeople had crossed the street before her as she idled in front of the town's central square the morning of her first scheduled shift, a couple with two small children. As she watched, the roly-poly baby was tossed in the air by the bespectacled mothman, peals of squealing infant laughter meeting her ears through the open window as the flailing bundle was caught. There had been a mothman that lived on her floor in the city for a short time, tall and slender and strangely attractive, with lovely smoke-colored wings and impossibly long fingers, but he'd kept to himself, his giant eyes lowering on the rare occasion they passed in the hallway, and she'd never worked up the nerve to speak to him. She'd watched as the couple reached the opposite sidewalk, where they were greeted by a petite goblin, clutching the hand of her own small, green-skinned child. *This is a nice place.* The thought had come to her unbidden, but the moment it crossed her mind, she had known it was true. *This is a nice place, and they wouldn't have a business that wasn't completely on the up-and-up operating right out in the open.*

"Everything you need is right here, so it's super simple. There's no uniform to buy, the scrubs are in the locker room. You just need to drop them in the laundry cart at the end of each shift, and you can change them throughout the day if you need to. There's nothing you need to buy, nothing you need to bring. Oh! You'll get a water bottle once you start, I keep mine in my locker so I don't forget it. That's really it! You just need to make sure you're following protocol with the clipboards and client labels and leave the rooms in the same condition you found them. Cleaning checks the sprayers every night, so you never have to worry about being out of something . . . it really is an easy job once you get into the groove of things!"

There were color-coded spray bottles containing different sanitizers on the wall outside of the collection room doorway: purple for the breeding bench, scented like oranges; green for the collection floor, with a strong, industrial odor. The scent did not linger, the girl assured her, drawing her attention to the mop clipped beside the sprayers. The bench needed to be sprayed down after each client left the room, and the floor given a cursory mop. If there was a *bigger mess* to clean—that bit relayed with a conspiratorially cocked eyebrow—she was to punch in the cleaning code into the keypad in the hallway, and flip over the red circle on the door before leaving, a signal to the janitorial associate who would respond and a warning for the next technician that the room was not ready for clients.

Violet nearly turned the same shade that her name implied when her brain caught up with what was implied by *a bigger mess*, before locating the instruction in her binder and drawing a rectangle around the four-digit code that would call for janitorial aid. *How often does **that** happen? Am I going to need to wear galoshes?*

"It's not that common an occurrence," the other woman continued as if she was able to divine thoughts. Violet had initially thought her to be another human, but the longer she spent trailing after the upbeat employee, the more she understood that her assumption was in error. The woman's wide, dark eyes were just that—wide and dark; a solid, inky pupil that bled into an iris of the same color, with no white sclera to break up the doll-like effect. She wore the uniform's surgical cap over her dark hair, but as the afternoon went on, Violet was able to make out twinned protrusions at her hairline, poking against the thin batting of the elastic cap, either horns or antennae, she deduced.

"It might happen once or twice in these early days, but you'll get the hang of it pretty quickly. The clients get upset if any of their collection is wasted, ya know? Every drop on the floor is a drop they're not getting paid for, and you're not going to want to deal with the mess . . . let's just say it's a *very* good incentive to not be slow with the nozzle."

She nodded, frantically scribbling notes in the margins of the training binder she clutched, despite the fact that each page featured brightly colored illustrations and step-by-step instructions. She'd always been a frantic note-taker in school, missing half the lecture in her haste to write down every single innocuous-sounding detail, and found herself slipping back into the bad habit now, in this strange place, in this strange town. The collection floor needed to be clinically clean; anything less and the bottles might be compromised, and there was nothing more important than the white-filled bottles, sloshing in their old-fashioned wire carriers.

"Hooking up the machine is the most intimidating part of the process, but it's really easy once you get the hang of it. You just want to make sure you're not cutting any corners now because when you're slammed in two months going from client to client, you'll be running on pure muscle memory, ya know? It's important to learn to do things the right way in the beginning."

Her throat seemed to seize as she swallowed, nearly choking at the girl's words. *How could she think that?! The machine . . . who cares about the stupid machine!* She'd been walked through the laundry facility, shown where the employee locker room was and where to find extra scrubs; led through the process of picking up her assigned rooms for the day and now a tour of the collection rooms themselves . . . but they'd still not covered the main aspect of the job, and Violet felt the reality of what would be expected of her sitting in the corner of the room like some great, hulking, horned shadow. The paper face mask evidently hid her exasperated expression, and the other woman turned away cheerfully, swinging open the door to the collection floor.

A circular work area lay ahead, anchored by the milking apparatus in the center of the room. A low bank of coolers and an empty table which would be filled with clipboards, were the room in use. A rack of shiny, chrome cylinders rested beside the table—the collection tanks, Violet understood immediately. Old-fashioned glass bottles, the kind she'd seen in roadside country stores and the most perverse detail of the farm's aesthetic, in her opinion, sat in neat lines on a shelf above an autoclave which they were to be sterilized within before being loaded into the machine. She did her best to pay attention, noting how the autoclave was started and the way the collection tanks were hooked into the milking machine and how she connected the hoses. Violet supposed the mechanical aspect to the job might, in fact, be intimidating, particularly the speed with which she was expected to execute the set-up . . . but she found herself surreptitiously glancing upwards every few seconds, her eyes finding the hole in the bench above her head every time her training partner turned away.

The collection floor sat half-a-level below the area the clients entered, a short staircase granting the collection associates access to the upper part of the room. The bench, from what she could see of it, reminded her of the twenty-minute massage chairs in the center of the mall back home, which self-consciousness had always kept her from patronizing. The bench above her had a similar design: a padded headrest and armrests, cannily placed braces for the sitter's legs to rest against, and a wide support for the torso. It was tipped forward at a more extreme angle, and the sheer size of the thing gave hint to the tremendous stature of the clients who would be resting there. The main differences were the thick upholstery cushioning . . . and, of course, the hole. Placed in the center of the bench's front supports, the opening gave clear access to the technician on the lower level, just before the chrome machinery in the center of the workspace, identical to those used on traditional dairy farms.

Violet wondered, as her hand reached out to lift one of the milking machine's nozzles, if the minotaurs would be able to see her below them as she worked, or if she would be completely hidden from view. Her mortification at the thought was, thankfully, well-disguised. She'd been worried that the cow-print apron and short-sleeved top worn by the technician in the video was the actual uniform, but reality proved to be much more sterile: the provided nursing scrubs were worn with a surgical cap, an isolation mask that covered the majority of her face, and sterile gloves. She had breathed a sigh of relief as she caught sight of herself in the reflection of the glass wall outside the locker room that morning—her identity was indecipherable.

The circumference of the nozzle in her hand was larger than that of a soda can, her fingers barely able to stretch around it, her nails not quite meeting as she lifted it for inspection. A silky interior met her fingers, highly textured medical-grade silicone, filled with bumps and nodules and ridges. Her training partner flipped the chrome-plated switch at the side of the collection unit then, and the machine whirred to life. Violet watched the hydraulic arm begin to move, pistoning up and down, causing the nozzle in her hand to buzz and hum, the percussive thump of the motor seeming to match the sudden pounding of her heart.

"Once you've got the tanks hooked into place and the client situated . . . " the other girl began, shrugging as Violet looked up. She was able to see the smile in the other woman's eyes, despite the paper mask that covered the majority of her face. "You just get to work. It's as easy as flipping a switch."

Her hand moved over the opening, fingers pressing into the silky-smooth interior once more, catching on the nodules within until she felt the suction of the machine, a rhythmic tightening, inhaling her fingers into the mouth of the nozzle. The light that came from above would be blotted out, she realized, when a hulking body covered the bench above her, the glow from the upper level currently afforded by the hole in the bench plugged with turgid male flesh, leaving her in shadow to handle the sucking nozzles below. The implications of the machine, of the pistoning suction, the interior texture and nodules, the *size* of the cylinder in her hand, the hole in the bench above her head . . . blood pounded in her ears and the room pitched, and Violet staggered away from the circular work area, gasping for air her lungs felt as though they'd been inexplicably deprived, as the trainer clicked the machine off.

"I know it's a lot," the other woman called out, once more seeming to discern her thoughts. "The clean-up, the machines, the checklists— it's all to remind us that this is a normal job, ya know? It's not any different than working at the blood banks or the organ trade-in places. Some facilities extract venom from snake people to make medicines, we extract this. It's no different."

She straightened, sucking in a long breath, wondering what kind of establishment traded in organs before shaking the unsettling thought away and pushed back her shoulders. "R-right. It's definitely not sex work."

"It's not, technically," the other woman went on, eyeing Violet dubiously. "There's a sexual element in it for the clients, obviously, and that's not even true for all of them. Some of them are just here to get paid. But . . . humans have a, let's say *different* view on what you call 'sex work' than a lot of us do. There are a lot of species that go through seasonal heats, did you know that? It's not just being horny, it's a medical handicap. Not everyone has the luxury of having someone at home to help them get through it. Being a heat helper is a real job, you know, and a lucrative one. 'Seasonal assistance positions,' they're called. There's a sexual element to it for the client in need of assistance, but it's more like . . . home health care, I guess. You'll see soon enough, it's not sexual for *us*, not any more than drawing blood is. Do you need to take a breather?"

No different than drawing blood. You're going to be good at this. "No, I-I'm fine. What's next?"

The girl eyed her speculatively for a long moment, the foreign appendages on her head twitching beneath the paper cap. *Definitely antennae.* Her doll-like eyes crinkled as she smiled before nodding. "Yep, I think you will be. C'mon, let's take a fifteen, you can grab a snack from the vending machines. Then we'll start some rotations, okay?"

The goal for every client is a plentiful, speedy collection. Violet felt her insides turn to jelly at the thought of seeing the collection process live in person already, but she squared her shoulders once more, nodding. She could do this. "Sounds good to me, I'm ready for it."

* * *

She was not, in fact, ready for it.

The first client of the day had been a towering minotaur of at least seven feet, and she'd gaped at the sight of him gazing down from the room's upper level, lazily pumping the erection that jutted from the opening of his pants, grateful for the mask she wore. His expression was cocky as he turned to undress fully before straddling the breeding bench, smirking over the side at the antennaed girl's announcement that a trainee would be observing that day.

"Well, you'd better train her up right. Give her a good demonstration of the proper *technique.*"

His entire body was covered in a spotted, short-haired hide of sable and cream, and his long member bore the same markings, Violet saw once he lowered himself to the bench, cock slipping through the opening. The spots on his shaft were interrupted by several thick veins, the markings fading as her eyes traveled up the stiff length, her mouth running dry at his wide, mid-shaft swell, ending in a light pink head the size of her fist, the deep slit at its tip already beading with moisture.

"This won't take long," he chuckled, groaning when the technician's oil-slickened hands gripped him, slickening his skin in a smooth glide. "I'm ready to burst as it is, this is two days of build-up."

She stepped closer as her training partner began stroking the long cock, wanting to ensure she was fully concealed beneath the bench . . . and wanting a better look, she admitted to herself. His balls indeed looked full to bursting, at least to her eyes, watching in fascination as his sac tightened as he was pumped, the twinned bulges the skin concealed raising slightly. *Pressure on the head,* she read, glancing down to his chart, and sure enough, the technician's hand had closed over the minotaur's cockhead then, pushing back the thick foreskin, her wrist moving in a figure-eight movement as she squeezed. Violet was certain she was blushing at the squelching sound made by the movement, but the minotaur above didn't seem to mind, letting out a deep bellow.

"Mmmm, you know that's what I like . . ."

When his hips began to pump against the upholstery, chasing his release with sharp thrusts, the other girl motioned meaningfully to the chrome-plated milking machine, nodding with a smile when Violet hesitantly reached out to flip the switch. The motor whirred to life, the piston within beginning to move.

"You want to pay attention to their cues," she said, once Violet had leaned in to hear her over the noise of the motor. "Once they start bucking, it's best to just turn it on, that way you're ready. In the beginning, you can turn it on as soon as you start, until you're comfortable judging. It's better to be too quick with the nozzle than too late."

When the antennaed girl passed her hand over the minotaur's swollen testicles, he jerked hard against the bench, grunting. "Get ready, new girl," he groaned out, his hips stuttering when the technician picked up the nozzle, sucking it over his dripping head in a teasing manner, "I'm about to blow, and you don't want to miss a drop."

The nozzle made several passes, his pink cock-tip disappearing and reappearing, a wet thread of his prerelease clinging obscenely to the lip of the silicone before it was worked over his shaft fully, and then it was all over. The minotaur arched against the bench, groaning something unintelligible just before he came, shaking against the upholstery and filling the bottle at the base of the collection unit with ropes of white, his hips hitting the bench with a terrifying force, over and over, culminating in a grunt of satisfaction as he slumped against the headrest, drained. The milk bottle, Violet noted with a trembling hand, was full.

"He's one of the Earners," the antennaed trainer explained after the cocky minotaur had risen and redressed, wishing her good luck with a wink that sent heat flooding to her cheeks, before leaving the room with a jaunty whistle. Violet watched her efficiently pull one of the bar codes from the clipboard, neatly affixing it to the front of the bottle before the label was scanned, the white-filled bottle placed on a small scale until the digital display flashed. *Accepted - 24 fl oz.* Twenty-four ounces, she thought to herself, gulping. She wondered over the puddle size twenty-four ounces would make, what a mess that might be to clean . . .

"Those are the clients that can account for every drop. Literally, they can pull on their balls and calculate exactly what they'll be making for the day, it's wild. You definitely don't want to be too slow with the nozzle with any of them!" Violet nodded, making a mental note, hoping she'd remember to add it to her binder. *Earners—be quick with the nozzle.* "So you need to put the sticky label from his file on the bottle, scan and weigh it, that's how they get paid," the trainer instructed, "and then this collection tank and hose get put on the conveyor, we don't have to do the cleaning, thank the goddess. You go over the sanitation checklist, I'm going to go grab the next file. We probably only have about fifteen minutes before the next appointment, so be quick about it."

She sprang into action, panicked at the thought of slowing down the schedule, slightly horrified over what she'd just witnessed, over what she'd be taking part in . . . and more than a little curious to watch it happen again. *You can do this, just think about the loft above the garage. What's worse?* Squaring her shoulders, Violet double-fisted the cleaning nozzles like a cowboy, already knowing the answer to that particular question.

Chapter 3

The rest of the week passed in a blur.

She had memorized her training binder backward and forward at that point, had watched and re-watched the training videos available on the company portal until she was able to anticipate every twist of the smiling, fox-faced woman's hands, could speak along with her verbal instructions, and knew exactly when the minotaurs on the video would groan and thrust, erupting into the nozzle of the collection unit. She had practiced setting up the rooms and running the autoclave, even though it technically wouldn't be a part of her daily duties; knew how to hook the collection units into the machine and affix the labels to the fronts of the milk bottles with one hand. The additional knowledge passed on by her training partner was invaluable, information not included in the binders, and she now knew the difference between the Earners and the Clockwatchers and casual clients, and had been slightly horrified to learn about the *Good Little Cows*.

"Did you tell her about the scrubs?" asked a middle-aged ogress, towards the end of her first week. Violet had settled into a routine for each day—she'd make the drive to Cambric Creek, her stomach a tangled bundle of nerves, cursing herself for not leaving early enough to stop at the little black-awninged coffee shop she passed in the town's center, arriving at the farm with just enough time to sit in her car and breathe herself back to a state of relative confidence. The job wasn't so bad, she thought, if one overlooked the work actually being done. The co-workers she'd met so far were friendly and welcoming and eager to offer pointers, and she was grateful for their experience.

"You'll want to check the file before you put on the scrubs," the ogress advised, pulling her own lime green top over her broad shoulders. "Sometimes they make requests."

"For the scrubs?"

"Mmhm. There's a denim overall print and an alpine milkmaid...I'm not saying they're all like that, but just, uh . . . be aware."

Kirime groaned in disgust, shoving her powder blue backpack into her locker with more force than necessary. The antennaed girl had been her training partner the entire week, introducing her to the other milking technicians and the janitorial staff, remaining cheerful and upbeat throughout and Violet liked her immensely.

"I'm sad to say it's true, Violet. You know how the Clockwatchers want to get in and out as fast as possible?"

Violet nodded with a gulp. The other techs had been teaching her the unspoken rules of the farm, the sort of information she'd not find in any of the manuals or videos. The Earners could account for every drop of semen they produced, practically earning a second income from their output. *Nice work if you could get it*, she thought privately. The Pop-n-Gos were the minotaurs who visited the farm infrequently, sometimes for the very first time, who were unprepared for the sensation of the sucking milking machine nozzles, ejaculating almost immediately and leaving the room just as quickly, unable to meet the tech's eye, no matter how they'd blustered when their pants were still on. The Clockwatchers tended to be businessmen, always on their way to somewhere else. The milking process was a transaction to those bulls, and they rarely vocalized on the breeding bench, remaining as still as they might have during a prostate exam in the doctor's office. They were brusque and slightly intimidating, and her least favorite type of client, she had decided in the few days she'd been observing on the collection floor.

"Well, there's another type of client to be aware of."

The ogress snorted, snapping the head-covering over her tightly-shorn hair. "The Good Little Cows."

"The Good Little Cows?"

Kirime nodded, making an expression that Violet had come to decipher as her version of an eye roll, or at least, as closely as she could approximate with her solid black sclera. "They really like to really push the fantasy of being 'milked.' It's a fetish thing for them, but they tend to be the very best tippers, so it's just something to tolerate. But!" she went on, raising her thin eyebrows and pointing at the ceiling, "the suits are serious about keeping everything professional, so if any client ever tries to push the envelope too far, you can end their session and report them and they won't be welcomed back."

"You'll get the occasional client who wants you to lick it," the ogress added helpfully, and Violet felt her stomach clench as both women groaned. "They'll be like 'this will go faster if you suck it, baby,' but it's almost always the Pop-n-Gos who say that, like they're not going to explode immediately anyway. And then we never see them again, so it doesn't matter," she laughed.

Violet echoed with her own weak chuckle, feeling queasy at the thought. She didn't want to be a part of these men's fantasies, wanted to be an invisible presence under the bench beneath them, wanted to tell herself she was performing a technical action no different than drawing blood—and more importantly—she wanted to believe it.

"Stop scaring her, Ruga," the antennaed girl admonished. "That almost never happens. And don't worry, I checked the files already, we don't have any Good Little Cows today."

Almost as if the ogress had spoken it into existence, the first client of the day was one of the Pop-n-go bulls, full of swagger, commenting that he hoped the impressiveness of his member wouldn't 'scare off the new girl.' When the nozzle was applied to his head, the green light on the machine illuminated almost immediately and the minotaur stiffened, shaking as though he'd been electrocuted against the bench above. He was silent as he dressed, thin tail swishing as he ducked out the door with his pants still unzipped, and she and Kirime dissolved into giggles, her panic over the morning's conversation forgotten.

It's fine, everything will be fine. At night, once she was back in her little Bridgeton apartment, she'd log onto the company portal and check her hours for the day, using the calculator on her phone to tally up each day's earnings, deducting taxes and the cost of gas and adding it the previous day's total, doing a giddy little dance around her kitchen at the growing balance. She couldn't remember the last time she'd earned so much money, the last time solvency was an actual possibility, and would tuck into bed with her tablet, scrolling through home decorating sites and recipes featuring luxury ingredients she'd never been able to previously afford. *You're going to be great at this and you're going to pay off your credit cards before the end of the year.*

Her ebullient confidence lasted through two more clients, both Earners, both easy and fast, a good start to the day, leading her down a path of self-delusion, overconfident that everything would stay this simple and rose-colored.

"Okay Violet, you're going to handle the next one, okay? I'll be right here, so you don't need to be nervous!"

All of her training, all of the videos and checklists and the handbook she memorized backward and forward, her confidence over the morning and her first week, the excitement over her future financial solvency and the fantasy shopping trips she'd taken in her mind; the promise of savings in the bank and her certainty that she'd be good at this job—it all dried up, blowing away like a scatter of leaves in an autumn breeze, leaving her legs as wobbly as a newborn foal as she entered the collection room at the other girl's encouragement. Somewhere, in the course of the last week, she'd lost sight of the reality that she was the one who would be administering the milkings; that she'd be a passive observer no longer. She'd become very comfortable trailing after Kirime, carrying the clipboards and springing into action when the tanks needed to be clicked into place and the labels affixed as if that would be the extent of her duties. *This* would be the reality of the job, she gulped, the end of her innocence.

Violet wasn't sure what she'd been hoping for as she entered the room, but her stomach sank at the sight of a broad, well-muscled back encased in a crisp, white dress shirt. The minotaur was already stepping out of his well-tailored pants and carefully placing them over the chair back, the glint of his heavy watch face catching the light, the clear markings of one of the Clockwatchers. *Maybe he'll be different,* she thought, staring up at the minotaur dumbly from the lower level. The short, silky-coarse hide that covered his body was the same color as the shaggy, pecan-brown hair that fell messily into his face, with huge, roan-colored horns pushing through it like weeds, stretching outward and to the sky. He was already partially erect, she saw at once. *Well, that'll speed things up, if nothing else . . .* Her jaw worked, a dozen different awkward greetings crowding her mind, leaving her tongue useless and her voice mute as the minotaur turned, the overhead light catching on the thick, gold ring spanning the width of his pink nose.

"I'm on my lunch break," he announced in a deep, resonant voice, cutting off her failed preamble before it had a chance to fully draw breath.

Her hope that he'd be friendlier than the typical Clockwatcher fizzled away as she nodded silently, still unable to force words from the throat. Fortunately, Kirime was, as she'd promised, right there. "That's no problem! We have a trainee working with you today, but I assure you we'll have you out the door in no time."

She'd never been under the table in the lead position before, Violet realized, feeling panicked claustrophobia grip her as the light above was blotted out when the minotaur swung his leg over the bench. His hooves scraped against the turf lining on the footrests as he settled himself into position, filling the opening in the bench with the thickest cock she'd ever seen, his wide hips sealing out the light completely. *There's a prime beef joke to be made here, I just know it.* She sucked in a breath, holding it for several seconds in an effort to steady herself, exhaling through her nose slowly. *You can do this, just remember the steps.* Her hands were trembling by the time she took up the clipboard, ensuring all necessary bits of information was filled in, completing the sanitation sweep, and ensuring the collection bottles were locked into the milking station. All that was left, she read on the checklist, was to start the milking machine and lube up her gloved hands.

Pecan brown at the base, the same shade as his short hide, fading until it bled into pink at the thick swell midway up his shaft, her hand was unable to span the circumference of him, obliging her to use both to slicken him with oil, all the way to the tip, the head still shielded by his foreskin. *You can't put your hand around him and he's not even really that hard, this is a chub for him!*

Her small hands were likely to be a detriment to the job, she thought as she reversed her motion, slowly pulling his foreskin back to reveal the bulbous, dark pink head, shiny-smooth with a deep, winking slit. One of the veins snaking up from the base was the same width as one of her fingers, and she traced it with the tip of her nail as she made one more pass with the lube, confident she could begin stroking him with no discomfort. *Time to get to work before he gets impatient.* Thinking of the training video, she tightened her grip. This bull was in a hurry, after all—she knew how to give a hand job, knew how to squeeze and stroke. *You can do this.*

The side of her pinky slid beneath the edge of his foreskin as she worked down the shaft, circling around his cockhead from within the protective layer of skin to ensure he was adequately slick, raising her head in surprise at the sharp intake of breath from above.

Violet paused, hoping she hadn't caused any discomfort, bracing herself for rebuke as she quickly pulled her hand back, but none came and the minotaur remained silent . . . although it seemed that he was breathing a bit harder. *He would say something if he doesn't like what you're doing, right?*

"Please just let me know if I'm using too much pressure," she called out hesitantly, having heard Kirime say similar things to clients brand new to the farm. "Or-or not enough pressure. Just, um, just let me know." A short grunt was her only response, and she shrugged to herself, gripping the turgid length once more. *He definitely responded to that, you weren't imagining it.* There was nothing on his chart, she read from where it was propped on the table before her—no preferences, no technician notes; nothing more than his initials and age and weight, followed by the eight-digit identification number and bar code, matching that of the adhesive label that she would affix to his bottle. No noted preference, but as she slipped her finger beneath the loose pucker of skin once more, the minotaur grunted again, his breath hitching when she circled around the flared underside of his still-sheathed cockhead, rubbing against the inside of the foreskin on another circular pass before sliding her pinky free and gently easing the skin back, exposing his head.

His cock had stiffened fully by then, a cord of steel within the solid length, and Violet marveled silently at his girth. It was not the biggest cock she'd seen over the course of the past week, but it was by far the thickest, fat and heavy in her slick hands. Using both, Violet pulled down his length, reversing once she reached the head, sliding her hands up his shaft to where his balls hung plump and full, tightening her grip and pushing into his root once she'd reached the base, an action that earned another one of those unexpected hitching breaths, and so she repeated it twice more. Once she'd established a stroking rhythm, she enclosed his cockhead in her fist, sliding over the pre-come he was steadily weeping by then, twisting and squelching until his hips bucked, a strangled hiss accompanying the action.

The Clockwatchers almost never displayed any tells, never showed anything but impatience and stoicism, and she *knew* it was inappropriate to feel a thrill over forcing a reaction from him, and even less so to register that thrill directly between her thighs, a tingle that ignited when he repeated the motion.

She'd lost track of how long she'd been pumping the huge cock by then, using one hand to twist over the exposed head, earning the occasional jerk from the big bull. The squelching of her lubed-up hands and the occasional sharp inhalations and stifled grunts from the minotaur above were competing with the sound of the milking machine, and when he began to subtly thrust his hide-covered hips against the padded legs of his chair continuously, Violet nearly missed the movement, expecting the over-the-top bucking that she'd witnessed from the other bulls all week. Subtle but unmistakable, the big bull pumped into her hands, chasing a victory she knew he'd catch. The thought of accidentally being splattered in a torrent of minotaur semen was enough to make her jump into action, briefly releasing the slickened, straining length to retrieve one of the sucking nozzles. Another half-groan escaped him as the bulbous head of his cock was sucked into the machine, the scrape of his hooves audible over the sound of the pistoning arm of the milker as she worked the nozzle down his thick shaft, knowing the hydraulic system would finish the job.

The smiling face of the fox-faced woman from the training video beamed from her mind then: *I like to continue providing manual stimulation at this point* . . . Violet swallowed resolutely, determined to do things right, before raising her hands to the huge testicles. Each one was the size of a large orange, the sac that encased them the same warm brown as his body. The seam that separated them seemed to draw in her finger like a beacon, and she traced it tentatively, earning a huff from above. The sound gave her confidence as she tested the weight of his balls, letting each rest heavily in her palms before rolling her slippery hands over them, squeezing as she did so. Another grunt as she squeezed, and then she released him for a moment, to ensure he appreciated the extra *stimulation*. Violet watched in fascination as his balls moved within their sac, tightening and pulling up to his body, her hands rising to meet them once more, tugging each gently, just a hint of stretch, and giving them another squeeze.

The reaction from above was immediate.

A groan he was unable to choke back, an increase in the movement of his hips, a telltale pulsing through his testicles as she pulled and rolled them, the sound coming again when the green light flared to life. She should have let go. Violet knew that; told herself she ought to do so immediately, but she was hypnotized by the way his heavy balls throbbed as he came, each spurt of his cock into the milking machine originating beneath her fingertips, and she began to squeeze them in time, helping him empty every drop.

The bottle was completely full when the light flicked to red and the suction of the machine quickly cut off. She was glad for the mask that covered the majority of her face, for she was certain she was flaming scarlet as she pulled the nozzle from his deflated cock, still fat and heavy, despite its softened state.

Taking care of the client so they could be on their way was the priority, she remembered, even over taking care of the collection bottle, and she turned to move into action before needing to be prodded. Warm cleansing wipes were used to remove excess semen from the clients' dangling members, which she'd witnessed being done more than a dozen times at that point, but that didn't prevent her stomach from somersaulting as she raised the wipe to clean the curiously responsive Clockwatcher, particularly when he shuddered as she gently tugged his retracted foreskin to swipe over his pink head, still sticky with his release. She didn't strictly need to bring another of the cloths to wipe clean the big testicles, swinging looser now that they'd been drained, but she told herself she was just being thorough, before giving them a final light squeeze.

Kirime's words about muscle memory taking over proved true as Violet deliberately turned her back on the upper level, not wanting to see the minotaur who'd caused such an inappropriate response as she squeezed her thighs together, focusing instead on the rest of her steps. *Cap and weigh the milk bottle, place in cooler; unhook the collection unit and disinfect the workstation.*

"First client down!" Kirime crowed once the used collection tank had been sent down the conveyor belt for disinfecting and Violet turned, relieved to see the upper portion of the room empty. "Congrats, the hard part is over!

The hard part indeed, she thought, her fingers still feeling the heft and weight of the minotaur. There was no time to reflect on the tingle between her thighs, as the next clipboard was pressed into her hands; one turning into six, and then she was pulling her last set of scrubs over her head, tossing them into the laundry cart in the locker room before she knew it. The rest of the day had passed in a whirl, several more Earners and a brand new client who seemed more nervous than she felt at that point. Violet blinked in surprise upon tapping her employee number into the tablet used for checking in and out for shifts, seeing a notation to visit the reception desk. She found herself in a short line behind two other employees, each collecting small, sky blue envelopes from the friendly receptionist. "Have a nice day!" the cheerful goblin called as she turned away from the counter, sliding the four envelopes bearing her employee number into her bag. She'd wanted to stop off at that little coffee shop she passed on her drive through town, wanted to peek into the intriguing shop windows and stroll around Cambric Creek's little downtown . . . but she was too distracted that day, too preoccupied, shifting behind the driver's wheel at a red light, unable to assuage the itch between her legs that desperately needed scratching.

* * *

It had been easy to put her official first client out of mind with the bustle of the day, but as she entered her apartment later that afternoon, kicking off her shoes and shedding her clothes as she moved through the rooms, the remembrance of that impossibly thick cock came back to her.

She'd planned on hauling her laundry down to the machines in the building's basement when she got home, wanted to make a recipe she'd found scrolling on the Thrifty Kitchen page, thought maybe she'd treat herself to ice cream that wasn't purchased from the bodega on the corner, but like her desire to explore Cambric Creek, her plans were set aside for a greater need. Instead, Violet detoured to her bedroom, flopping down on top of her comforter and slipping her hand into her panties, the last item of clothing she still wore. She was unsurprised to find herself already wet, the tingling arousal she'd felt hours earlier returning full force now that she could address it.

The panties were kicked off, dropping to the floor beside the bed as she dragged her fingers through her folds, coating them in slick and rubbing the moisture over her tingling clit, teasing back and forth until the swollen bud protruded from its hood, needy for more stimulation.

The fingers on her other hand curved, approximating the way they'd stretched around the minotaur's girth, remembering the way she'd tightened her grip to squeeze the rigid length. She could almost feel the heavy weight of him, the solidity and thickness of him, the way his cock hardened to steel in her hand. Violet gasped, circling over her clit in earnest then, remembering that sharp little intake of breath he'd made when she'd slipped her finger inside his foreskin, his grunt of pleasure when she'd squeezed his meaty balls. She arched, sliding a finger into herself, adding a second and a third, trying to imagine how a cock that thick would fill her, would stretch her far beyond what she'd ever taken before. She'd had a few well-endowed partners over the years, but she was hardly a size queen and couldn't imagine what it would feel like to be that *stuffed*.

She thought of the slow way he'd pumped his hips, his groan when she'd worked the sucking nozzle over his cockhead, the way she'd been able to feel the building tightness and pressure in his huge testicles, the way they'd begun to throb with his orgasm just before the first eruption of his release into the milking machine. Her hips left the bed, thrusting upwards, remembering

33

the way he'd continued to pulse as he came, each spatter of white against the side of the glass bottle felt in the way his balls throbbed in her hands. Violet clenched around her own fingers, reaching her peak as she remembered the way it had felt *feeling* his orgasm, and she was positive the rhythmic convulsions that gripped her shared the same pulsing cadence.

When it was over, she stared up at the ceiling, inhaling and letting out a ragged breath. *What the fuck was that?* She didn't know why she'd been so affected by the Clockwatcher, why him, among all the other minotaurs she'd worked on that day, amongst all those she'd observed over her training? It made no sense, was completely inappropriate, and she shook the thought of him away as she struggled to sit, hands scrabbling at the bedding for purchase. *He's a client, just a nameless, faceless client, and you'll probably never even see him again.*

One head-clearing shower later, her Thrifty Kitchen recipe started and her laundry set for a double spin cycle, Violet remembered the cerulean envelopes slipped into the front pocket of her backpack as she'd left the farm. The family above her was doing another one of their stomping jamborees as she dropped into the chair at her battered little kitchen table. She'd had seven clients in total that day, four of them leaving her tips: a conglomeration of crumpled bills, tens and twenties, enough to justify getting that gourmet coffee and a guilt-free lunch to go with it . . . and one crisply folded hundred, perfectly smooth with sharp edges. There was only one client it could have come from, only one client that day who'd sported the tailoring and expensive accessories of the Clockwatchers. She could imagine the bill being pulled from a billfold or money clip that cost as much as her rent, could almost see the minotaur with the messy hair folding it in perfect thirds before grunting in response to the receptionist's cheerful farewell.

She could pay her cellphone bill, Violet considered, without needing to carry the monthly late fee that had become her norm, the money saved from the late charge being applied to her student loan bill or the credit cards she'd been living off of, a tiny bit of ground made, but made nonetheless. *An acknowledgment of being quick and thorough, that's all.* She'd trained hard, had watched her videos and studied her binder, and the tips earned were a result of her hard work and nothing more, she reminded herself repeatedly through the evening, pushing thoughts of the Clockwatcher aside. When she fell into bed, hours later, she pushed them away once more, willing sleep to find her without tossing and turning all night.

She needed to be fresh for work the next morning.

II

Part Two

Chapter 4

I f a job's worth doing, it's worth doing well

How many times had she been lectured over the years by her parents and teachers with those words? Schoolwork, chores, a performance in the school play...Her mother would flap her hands and pace, repeatedly asking if she was ready for her quiz, knew her lines in the play, had checked over her choir robe. *If a job's worth doing, it's worth doing well, dear!* Was it any wonder that she'd taken it to heart?

It had been more than three weeks since she'd completed training at Morning Glory Farm and each day she strove to do her job well—a metric that was easily measured in old-fashioned milk bottles, filled to the brim. *A plentiful, speedy collection* had become her mantra, and each day she sought to increase her bottle count from the day before, besting her personal record, week over week.

When she learned about the cash bonus to the most productive milking associate, awarded on a monthly basis, her competitive streak flared to life, making the calculations on how she'd be able to double her credit card payments with the winnings and vowing to take the top prize at least once. She'd encountered several of the Good Little Cows at that point, had become proficient at getting the Clockwatchers out the door quickly, and laughed with decreasing awkwardness as the predictable jokes and casual banter of the Earners. Her tips were modest but appreciated, a nice little bonus that she saved for groceries, allowing her paychecks to be reserved for rent and bills. There'd been no repeat of the heat that had gripped her after her first solo run, not so much as a shiver of desire as she worked on client after client, bull after bull, every day. *That probably happens to everyone at first.*

The daily commute had proved not to be so terrible, and Cambric Creek beckoned her with its odd little shops and plethora of restaurants, rolling park and quaint little bandstand. The previous week she'd stopped at a little green market set up in the corner of the big park she drove past, stocking up on some fresh fruit and vegetables for the weekend, ecstatic that she was able to treat herself to such a luxury. She had seen sleek-feathered harpies and towering lizardmen, bulging with muscles; shaggy-haired centaurs and more goblins and trolls than she could count, and she was busting to learn about each of them—their food, their cultures, how everyone seemed to get along so seamlessly in the vibrant little community. She was settling in, Violet thought happily. *See? This job really was a lifeline.* She should have known then that her blind optimism was steering her towards an unseen cliff.

"Hold on, Violet! This one's yours . . ."

She turned with a furrowed brow as Magda held out an impatient hand, motioning to her stack of clipboards. The big orc was not her favorite co-worker. Brusque and somewhat impatient, Magda was in charge of organizing each day's schedule: ensuring each appointment slot had a technician assigned, that there was room on the schedule for the occasional walk-in, rotating technicians around the rooms in a way that gave the janitorial department plenty of time to stay on top of cleanliness and the set-up team adequate time to have the rooms ready for use. Violet recognized it was an important job and likely a stressful one, considering all the moving pieces involved, but the beetle-woman who worked aside Magda in the same capacity managed to be friendly.

The morning had already been harried. She'd been trying a new method of washing her dark brown curls, which entailed not washing them at all. All of the websites said a gentle conditioning was all she needed, that her hair would thank her and she'd reap the benefit of soft, bouncy ringlets. Violet didn't know how long it took to get to the soft and bouncy stage, but as she'd stared at herself in the mirror that morning: too-pale from never getting out of her apartment, slightly pear-shaped, the curls framing her face looking neither soft nor bouncy and an oily sheen at the top of her head, she determined that she seemed to be indefinitely trapped in the greasy bird's nest phase, one which was not discussed on the websites, and she couldn't abide leaving the house for one more day with an itchy, oily scalp.

The unplanned-for shower had set her back, forced to forgo breakfast as she hurried out the door, her wet curls still bound in the sodden t-shirt she used to dry them, arriving at the farm with only a few minutes to pull on a set of lavender scrubs and grab her files. She could still feel damp hair clinging to the back of her neck, as she returned to where Magda stood, wondering if the file being added was one of the Good Little Cows. *That's probably what she's doing, adding one to your stack, and you won't even have time to change scrubs.* Violet watched in confusion as the stern-voiced orc shuffled through the clipboards she'd handed back, squinting at the files before pulling one out, replacing it with one that bore a purple sticker on the side of the client label.

"Koveh! Take this one."

The nervous young man that had been in her training class turned in panic as Magda barked, quickly catching the clipboard she launched at him as if it were a shot put challenge, hunching as he did so to keep his own files from dropping, scampering out of the prep room as soon as he recovered his footing.

"What—what is this?"

"A request." The orc wrinkled her nose, as if Violet's question was particularly stupid, despite the fact that she was only learning about requests at that very moment. "You need to check for those before you just take your stack, you know, that could have screwed up the schedule for the whole day if I didn't catch it."

"That's not her job, Magda," Kirime cut in, appearing from the locker room doorway. "That's not any of our jobs. That's *your* job. *You* didn't catch the request. What you meant to say was 'sorry I missed this, I'll make sure to check the files over more completely!'"

Magda scowled, opening her mouth to reply, but Kirime had already linked her slender arm with Violet's, turning them out the door before the orc could fully draw breath.

"She's so full of it," the black-eyed girl said cheerfully, once they'd turned down the cool blue hallway. "Don't let her boss you around or blame you for stuff like that. Organizing the schedule isn't our job and she knows it."

"What—what does a request mean?"

Kirime shrugged, turning to go up a separate corridor with her own armload of files. "It means a client put in a request at reception. A request is just a request, it's not a guarantee. You won't get them very often, most clients don't even think of doing so. They don't know when we work and that information isn't divulged by the desk, so it's a roll of the dice for them, but they were happy enough with you that they asked!" She beamed, antennae twitching beneath her cap. "Don't worry, you don't need to change your schedule or anything. If you happen to be working when they come in, the request is honored. Otherwise," she shrugged, making a 'they get what they get' motion. "If they go through the trouble of putting in a request they usually tip well, so that's something to look forward to at least!"

Violet forced her lips into a smile, attempting to disguise the spike of nerves she felt at the revelation and the way her stomach flipped. There were more than a dozen clients who could have been responsible for a request, she told herself, any number of bulls who might have been satisfied enough with her clumsy, novice moves . . . but as they turned up their separate hallways lined with doors leading to the milking room floors, the apprehension within her grew, a wave of anxiety lapping at her heart.

"Have a good morning, Violet! Maybe we can grab coffee later!"

Kirime's parting was bright and Violet waved, hoping the antennaed girl's words would be prophetic as she tamped back the anxiousness she felt over that ominous purple sticker, but the already rushed morning proved to be anything but good.

Her first appointment of the day had been one of the Earners, straightforward and easy, but the second appointment was not. She had hooked the collection tanks into place more times than she could count at that point, and had mastered the twist-and-click motion needed to lock the heavy cylinders into the base, but as she stood beneath the upholstered bench, the minotaur waiting above, she could not make the tank cooperate. The minutes seemed to tick by as she struggled, the threading on the tank refusing to find purchase, her face heating. *Don't cry. Do NOT cry. If you cry, you'll never be able to show your face here again.*

"Does it need to go counter-clockwise?" he called out, leaning over the edge of the bench to peer down where she struggled. "You probably need to go in at an angle, sweetheart."

"I am," she gritted, not needing the extra sugar–baby–sweetheart bullsplain-

43

ing that day. Turning with a grunt of her own, Violet pulled a fresh tank from the rack, holding her breath as she tilted it into place . . . feeling it click in immediately. "There we go," she said weakly, attempting to channel some of Kirimie's effortless cheer and failing utterly. "Sorry about the hold-up, we can get started whenever you're ready!"

The incident seemed to have set her up for a free fall of bad luck the rest of the day. The bottle label was missing from the second appointment's clipboard, something she should have caught at the beginning of the session, *would* have caught had she not been running late from the disastrous first appointment. Something *Magda* should have caught, she thought furiously, racing to the intake desk to retrieve the missing label once the minotaur had left, running back to the collection room to affix it to the bottle before jogging to her next appointment. The only constant had been the friendly understanding from the endless line of bull men. The minotaurs waved off her tardiness, assured her she was doing fine, that bad days happened. It had lifted her spirits, distracting from the bad day until the purple sticker on the next clipboard, her second last of the day, brought her nerves back to crash around her like a wave breaking on a rocky shore.

She recognized his broad back immediately.

The dress shirt he wore had a subtle mint striping, setting off the russet highlights in his messy hair, which still fell into his face, as it had that first day. He'd not yet removed his pants, giving her a view of the way the fabric strained around his bulging thighs and well-rounded backside, thin tail swishing as he undid his fly, pausing when he turned to face her.

"How are you today?"

She'd not had a chance to appreciate his voice on that first day, as nervous as she'd been, but now the baritone resonance of it made her quake, still on that unsteady shore, waves of anxiety forming foaming white caps, the crash of which would certainly send her off her feet. There was a sharp edge of control in that voice, present even in the benign greeting, as though he weren't so much inquiring into her day as he was demanding she give him a report.

"I'm well," she forced out a beat later. "It's nice to see you again."

Violet suffered a moment of heart-clenching panic, wondering if she'd broken some social contract of non-acknowledgment, but he'd only nodded, the scrutiny of his chocolate-brown eyes pinning her to the spot, in danger of being overtaken by the undertow in her mind until she turned away, moving to set up her station. Once again, she found herself glad for the paper mask that hid the heat burning up her face.

"Actually . . . I suppose I'm well enough," she corrected, feeling marginally more secure once she had the shield of the breeding stocks between them. "This has been a disaster of a day. I had a piece of machinery that wouldn't cooperate this morning, and it set me behind schedule for the whole afternoon." His little huff made her bite her lip, and she listened to the rustle of him stepping from his pants. She wondered if his hooves ever caught on the hem of the legs, or if his tail ever got caught up in the seat, pressed against his round ass instead of slipping through its designated opening, questions that would go forever unanswered. "And before all that, your file almost didn't make it into my rotation for the day."

"So does that make me the origin of all your bad luck?"

Her eyes raised in surprise to the bench above her, but the Minotaur had not yet approached. *I guess he's not on his lunch break today.* She never expected conversation from any of the Clockwatchers, and the slight levity in his deep voice was a curiosity. "Well, I wouldn't go that far," she laughed hesitantly, "but I'm crossing my fingers that the last client of the day doesn't have any complications."

"Well, then we'd best get started so you're not late to your last appointment." It was unmistakably a command, and she jumped to comply, pulling a tank from the rack and deftly clicking it into place. "I'll try to time my inconveniences for later in the day next time."

Violet held her breath as his shadow moved over the opening in the bench, his big leg swinging over, listening for the scrape of his hooves on the turf and anticipating the moment when he would fill the hole . . . but nothing happened. The light from overhead continued to shine down uninterrupted, the shadow of the minotaur's horns casting down as he straddled the bench.

"Are you still in school?"

There was a slightly suspicious edge to the question, and she knew she ought not to answer it, despite the way her mouth opened to comply immediately. Giving out personal information to the clients was not advisable, blurring the edges of the professional distance the milking associate maintained from their lower level, but there was something about the way he asked, something in the way he held back from settling against the bench . . . Violet couldn't decide if he was trying to determine if she was an actual adult, perhaps feeling guilty over the fact that he'd evidently enjoyed the way she'd milked him enough to request her again, or if he was subtly insulting her, implying that he hoped she was pursuing an education so that this sort of job wouldn't be necessary. *That's what he thinks.*

"I'm not," she heard herself answer, sucking in a steadying breath before continuing. "I finished grad school over a year ago. Just waiting for a job in my field that actually pays the bills now." He grunted in response, her answer obviously satisfying the unknown subtext of his question, for a moment later she heard the creak of the upholstery as he leaned forward, and her hands twitched in anticipation. She could still feel the weight of him in her palms, even now, despite the number of bulls she'd handled since then.

"It's difficult out there right now," he said, his deep voice a sympathetic murmur as he shifted against the bench until he was comfortable. "Especially if you're just entering the marketplace. Entry-level isn't what it used to be."

"It's definitely not. Fortunately, this place was hiring, and I saw the ad at the perfect time."

"They treat you well here?"

He'd paused his movements again, and Violet huffed in slight impatience. He really *was* going to make her late for the next appointment at this rate. "They do. Very fair pay, full benefits. I couldn't ask for more."

"That's good," he mumbled, hooves scraping the back of the bench at last. "That's good to hear. They're extremely generous to clients, it's a relief to hear they treat the employees as well . . . I suppose I should let you get started."

Time seemed to move in slow motion as he settled his weight against the bench, his cock filling the hole and blotting out the light, heavy balls swinging. He was already hard, Violet observed, biting her lip. *Hard* hard, fully erect and already pearling pre-come. She wondered if their brief conversation had turned him on, if it was the knowledge that she wasn't some barely legal uni student that put his mind at ease and made his cock hard, wondered if his erection had stiffened and grown in anticipation of her stroking him again as he sat straddling the bench, his big balls contracting in need with her just underneath. *He requested you. Requested this.* He'd enjoyed the way she'd milked his balls dry enough to put in a request for her at the desk, she reminded herself, and she wasn't going to let him regret it.

The pearlescent bead of moisture glistening from the eye of his cocktip drew her like a magnet, her fingertip pressing into it, spreading it over the smooth pink of his head before pushing into the slit once more, earning a ragged breath from above.

"Just let me know if this is too much pressure," she murmured, her thumb and index finger meeting in a circle, sliding over his head. The only response she received was a brief sigh as she began to massage over his head with the lubed ring of her fingers, his foreskin moving easily beneath her hands. The response to slipping her pinky into the loose pucker of his foreskin, pulled back over his head, was expected—a barely perceptible groan, but no pulling away. Like the last time, she slid the pad of her finger against the nerve-ending-packed sheath, circling his cockhead. He jerked when she rubbed against his frenulum, a choked groan escaping when she persisted, back and forth, slipping her pinky free and using the loose skin to twist over his head, a constant motion she kept up until he made a noise deep in his throat, a growl of pleasure that he swallowed down, his thick fingers curled around the edge of the bench above, digging into the upholstery as though it might help him keep his grip on his rapidly dissolving composure, and Violet wasn't sure if she was elated that she'd been able to wring the sound from him or annoyed that he refused to give up control.

The weight of his cock was a delicious heft, heavy and solid in her hands as she began stroking his shaft from root to tip, pressing into the base on her downstroke and teasing his slit every time she twisted over his head, using both hands to move in a constant corkscrew, pulling him with increasing pressure, imagining that she'd be able to pull his big body right through the

hole in the bench, her hands moving in a constant pattern, one over the other
. . .

He was unable to hold in his groan then, deep and almost pained-sounding, as if he were dragging a burdensome weight uphill, lamenting the exertion of keeping it aloft, the sound sending a bolt of excitement to her own sex until her knees began to shake. She was unsurprised when he began to push against the bench, the same constrained movement as he'd displayed the first time, so different from the wild bucking she'd grown accustomed to from the other clients. Instead, this minotaur moved his hips in a deliberate, slow thrust, grunting as he did so, and rather than immediately releasing him to apply the nozzle, Violet loosened her grip slightly and spread her hands on his shaft, one around his head and the other around his base, flush against his big balls, allowing him to pump into the ring of her fingers.

She wondered if this was what it would be like to be fucked by the big bull: a slow, solid pounding, deep and exquisite, each slam of his wide hips filling her completely, a thought that made her face heat in mortification at the same time that she flooded with arousal. *What is wrong with you?! This is a client!* Violet knew her inner voice was right; that this train of thought was completely inappropriate, but she had no doubt that she would be dripping by the end of his session. *You'll be able to slide out of the room at this rate!*

The minotaur continued to fuck into the tight ring of her hands, his heavy balls slapping the back of her wrist with every thrust, his deep moan a strangled, half-swallowed thing. *Enough, you need to stop this. A plentiful, speedy collection . . .* She remembered back to the very first client she'd observed when she was still shadowing Kirime and the way the antennaed girl had used the nozzle to tease the spotted bull, the braggadocios Earner. The minotaur above her jolted when she did the same, passing the sucking mouth of the nozzle over his streaming cockhead several times, jerking each time she teased over him, pressing his head in and out of the textured opening before pulling back.

The amount of pre-come he was dripping was enough to cover her hands with no additional lube needed, and Violet considered that between the two of them, they might flood the room. *What the fuck is wrong with you?! Just finish him off and be done!* He hissed when she worked the nozzle down his cock at last, her hands immediately raising to his full testicles, unable to keep herself from cupping them and feeling their heavy weight against her palms, her fingers hugging them in greeting. His hips began to rock in earnest when she began to rub and squeeze, pulling her thumb and forefinger down the seam to separate them in their sac, pulsing them in time when they began to throb, his orgasm building in her hands.

He lowed as he came, a noise that could only come from a minotaur and one she'd never heard from any of the other Clockwatchers, deep and resonant in his rich voice as the green light flared to life on the machine, the hydraulic pump sucking on his head, slurping up his release more efficiently than any mouth could dream of attempting, and a fresh explosion of excitement exploded between her legs at the thought. She imagined the absolute *mess* his fat cock would make if it were permitted to erupt freely, for the twenty-four-ounce bottle was full to the brim when he sagged boneless against the bench, the machine clicking off and the motor whirring to a stop. He plopped wetly from the opening when she released the nozzle, swinging free and he grunted again. *Not so in control now.*

You shouldn't work on him anymore, you need to ask Kirime what you need to do, what you need to say, how you can make sure you don't get his file in your rotation. She knew the voice in her head was right, knew it was inappropriate to be thinking of a client this way, that it was unprofessional and likely grounds for dismissal . . . but when he spoke again, after she'd gently cleaned his spent cock and squeezed his balls one final time, Violet found herself pushing the voice aside.

"One more after this then? The slot after this one is your last for the day?"

"Yes," she answered, peeling off her gloves, smeared in his pre-come and oil. She didn't know how he managed to sound so collected and commanding already, his pants already on and zipped, pressed dress shirt tucked into the waistband neatly. Her legs were still trembling as she turned to face the upper level, taking in the broad set of his shoulders and the sharp cut of his horns through his messy hair. He was slimmer than many of the bulls who came through the milking room, and the lack of excess bulk made his sculpted biceps stand out beneath the material of his shirt, the tumble of pecan-colored hair over his forehead giving him a surprisingly boyish appearance. She'd never dated a non-human before, but it was impossible to deny that this minotaur was exceedingly attractive. "Thirty minutes after your appointment time for today would be my last spot of the day." *Who is it hurting? It's just a fantasy. You haven't gotten laid in forever, that's all this is.*

"Well . . . I'll have to keep that in mind. I hope my bad luck doesn't follow you home."

It was just a fantasy, she told herself once the room was cleaned and the minotaur long gone, heading to her last appointment, now fifteen minutes behind schedule. But then again, she hadn't had any inappropriate thoughts about any of the other clients. *Not like this one.*

Not like him at all, she thought, smiling at the black and white bull waiting for her in the last room of the day. The rest of the clients were a faceless void, and that was the way it was meant to be, she knew. *It's not like anything will happen. Just let things be.*

Three cerulean envelopes waited for her at checkout, and she didn't need to wonder which client had left her the sharply creased hundred dollar bill. *That's all this is, a transaction. Stop making more of things than they are.* Once again, Violet knew the voice in her head was right, but as she dropped back on her bed, safely ensconced in her apartment, her fingers slid over her aching clit, her velvet folds still dripping in her earlier arousal. It was the big bull with the messy hair she thought of when she retrieved her vibrator from her nightstand, trying to approximate the slow, deep, deliberate thrust of his hips.

She wondered if he would still be as assertive as he fucked her, keeping his composure and rutting her slowly as she melted to a puddle beneath him, feeling the weight of his cock and the slap of his balls, falling to pieces, completely at his mercy. It was the deep moan he made when he came she thought of as she reached her peak, clenching around the entirely-too-narrow vibrator, wishing it possessed his astounding girth as she keened, trying to imagine the mess twenty-four ounces would make of her sheets.

Chapter 5

"Pumpkin, I'm just so happy to hear you found something and you're doing well. You know we worry about you all alone up there in the city!"

Her mother's voice was tinny and distant through her low-quality Bluetooth headphones, and Violet considered that replacing them might need to jump the priority line over luxury vegetables. Her explorations around Cambric Creek had been tentative so far and completely restricted to her brief lunch break. There was a green market that set up on Wednesdays in the parking lot just up the road, which she'd taken advantage of several times since starting at the farm, relishing in the fresh produce, but not sounding as though she was having a conversation from the bottom of a well might be more important than fresh mesclun and radishes for dinner.

"You don't need to worry about me," Violet reminded her mother, knowing it was no use, as she was a worrier by nature. "It's been going really well so far. I'm actually able to start paying back my loans now, so you know . . . light at the end of the tunnel eventually."

She listened with half an ear as her mother made noises about her taking out so many loans, bemoaning the fact that it had been necessary in the first place. In front of her, a waifishly slender troll prepared her order of the barista's special. The coffee shop was down the street from the farm, nestled between businesses in a strip mall, and she'd been overjoyed to find it, stepping over the threshold with her heart thumping in her mouth, nervous over her first official trip into a non-human business . . . but the shop had been empty, save for the bored-looking troll behind the counter, a satyr who never looked up from his cellphone, and a hunched, hyena-faced man sitting near the window.

The coffee was her reward for the messy start to the day, necessitating changing her scrubs after the second client and punching in the cleaning code for the very first time. The bull had been younger than the normal farm client, maybe a bit younger than herself, and had seemed jittery from the moment she'd entered the room. He'd fidgeted as she took her place beneath the table, his long cock already purple at the tip, twitching before she'd even lubed her gloves.

"That means he likes you," he laughed nervously, and Violet sighed, assuming he'd be a Pop-n-Go client once the milking nozzle was applied.

"Just try to relax. Let me know if it's too much pressure."

He'd groaned when she slickened him with the oil, panting when she began to stroke. His pants had turned to whimpers as she brought one hand over another, reminding herself that this might actually be the least sexy job in the world, when only several minutes into his milking and without a single thrust of warning, he moaned long and loud, his cock erupting, coating her chest in ropes of his release, coming on her and on the floor, and nowhere near the milking machine.

"You haven't even told us what you're doing! Aunt Gracie was so excited to hear you found a good job, you need to call her and tell her all about it!"

She considered what her elderly great-aunt might say in response to hearing her surrogate granddaughter was professionally tasked with making minotaurs ejaculate, that she'd gone stomping back to the locker room that morning coated in a ridiculous amount of bullman semen, and decided it was a conversation best avoided. "It's a pharmaceutical company, mom," she cut in, attempting to quash a prolonged explanation. "I'm working with clients at a pharmaceutical company, it's hardly glamorous. But it doesn't need to be, because it's going to pay the bills. Did I tell you it's out in the suburbs? If I'm still here when my lease runs out, I might move closer to save on gas."

Her mother's exclamation of relief was expected, and Violet congratulated herself on changing the conversation's direction. "That's wonderful! We're so proud of you, pumpkin, and I think moving out of that awful city is an excellent idea. I forgot to mention . . . Carson from the up street? The

Tinsleys? Well, he's just moved back home. His mother was just telling me last week how happy she is to have him while he gets back on his feet after the divorce, you know. He grew up to be *very* handsome, Violet. Maybe the next time you're home for a visit the two of you could go for coffee and catch up."

Violet didn't need to tax her imagination to picture the smug look she knew had crossed her mother's face, the same one she always assumed when she thought she'd come up with a fantastic idea, regardless of how ill-thought the idea actually was. *Divorced before thirty and needs to move back home, as if that's something to aspire to.* The cup placed in front of her by the troll had a murky appearance, and she frowned. "Mom, I've got to get back, I'm just on my lunch break."

"Oh, of course! We're so proud of you, Violet. Call us on the laptop when you can, we want to hear all about it, okay?"

The diatomaceous earth in the barista's special gave the drink a chalk-like texture and mucky taste, even less appealing than the burnt coffee from the expensive chain near her apartment, and she only managed to choke down half the cup on her walk back to the farm before giving up. Her mother's less than subtle hint about her old junior high sweetheart rankled in her mind as she walked, and Violet scowled. She didn't *want* to move back home, didn't want to go back to the cookie-cutter middle class human neighborhood where she'd grown up, regardless of what her mother wished. It had been a looming possibility before the job at the farm, but now that she was actually starting to turn the corner off destitution alley, she was loath to think of going back, and the milquetoast human with whom she'd made mud pies as a child did nothing to sweeten the deal, despite what her mother hoped for. *You're not moving back and that's that. Time to focus on work.*

There was a purple stickered file waiting for her, and her stomach had twisted and flipped from the moment it was added to her stack that morning. It had been two weeks since she'd seen the Clockwatcher, and true to his word he'd booked the last appointment slot of the day, giving her seven hours to think about what might happen that week—imagining how witty she'd be, what their conversations might consist of and if it might arouse him, as it apparently had the previous week, if they'd have another conversation at all. She didn't make a habit of making small talk with any of the other clients, after all, and they never seemed inclined to do so on their own.

"I trust you're having a better day this week? I'd hate to think I was a harbinger of bad luck for you."

Violet didn't know what it was about him—the rigid set of his shoulders or the way his voice reminded her of a thunderclap, deep and matter-of-fact, or maybe a combination of the two, encased in his well-tailored business attire—but a shiver moved up her back as her stomach flipped and her legs nearly turned to liquid, heated by the fire he ignited between her thighs. *Hey, this isn't a sexual job, remember?* She'd always been a sucker for authority, eager to impress her professors and supervisors with quick compliance, and she suspected if this sharp-voiced minotaur barked an order for her to climb the short staircase and kneel before him, thick cock hanging obscenely over the unzipped fly of his pants, she'd have dropped to the ground without a moment of hesitation.

As it was, the big bull loomed from the center of the upper room, looking down over her. His shirt that day was a pale blue, well-pressed and tidy; his trousers a slate grey, and his hair as messy as ever. Violet did her best to suck in a slow breath through her nose, not betraying the butterflies she'd felt all morning and afternoon. "It's been a very good day, actually. I had a cancellation earlier, so I finally had a chance to grab a coffee that didn't come from our break room, and the rest of the day's been pretty easy. Maybe you're a good luck charm in this time slot."

He chuckled at that, deep and rumbling, and the butterflies within her took wing once more. "Well, that's a relief. I'd hate to go back to the other place across town, but I'd be forced to make the sacrifice if you were still slipping on banana peels and missing files every week."

She sputtered in mock outrage, her laughter ringing through the circular room, raising her head from the tank she'd hauled off the rack just in time to see the corners of his mouth lift slightly, the barest hint of a smirk. "I don't recall ever saying *any*thing about banana peels."

His shoulders lifted in a small shrug as his pants fell. "I used my imagination. In any case I'm relieved to hear it."

The bench creaked overhead as she hooked the tank into place, quickly reviewing the readiness checklist. She tried to imagine him swinging a leg over the bench, his thick thighs squeezing the upholstery as he waited for her. She had only ever glimpsed the clients from the thighs up, and wondered what the rest of his legs looked like: if he had sharp, glinting hooves or if they were neatly filed; buffed to a shine or scuffed from activity.

There had been a satyr in line ahead of her that morning at the little coffee shop in the shopping plaza up the street from the Farm's campus, and Violet had done her best to be discreet as she looked over his lower half, imagining that he would be at least close in composition to a minotaur. To her fascination, the satyr's jeans had ended just above his jutting hocks, and she'd wondered if the messy-haired minotaur's bespoke dress pants did the same. The satyr's black hooves had been scuffed grey around their edges, and she'd been unable to imagine her unnamed minotaur's looking the same. Everything about him seemed too controlled for that, too polished and austere. *Well . . . except that messy hair. Besides, you're acting like you know anything about him. And why are you trying to flirt with him!? It's one thing to get off thinking about his junk, you don't need to wind up with a crush. That's completely unprofessional.*

She scowled at her inner monologue, shaking the sensible voice away. *Shut up. We're just having fun, it's a conversation, not a proposal.* The minotaur's previous words had sparked a question in her mind, and she voiced it then, taking her place beneath the table. "There's another place like this? These sorts of places are . . . common then?"

"Mhm. There's one in Bridgeton, right by the history museum. I've been to that one and the one in Starling Heights, but that place doesn't compensate enough to make the drive worth it."

"I live in Bridgeton!" she exclaimed in awe, trying to imagine what building housed the milking facility, only realizing belatedly that she was sharing more personal information. "I go past the history museum a few times a week, I can't believe I didn't know it was there!"

He huffed again, that deep chuff that wasn't quite a laugh. "It's in the same building as the flower shop with the big window displays. I used to live in Bridgeton and it was convenient then, but I wouldn't want to go back there now. Not as nice as this place, or as selective."

"I don't know why I thought this place was unique. So do all minotaurs know about this?"

"Oh, they know alright. Most bulls do it, and if they haven't yet, believe me, they're thinking about it. There's no reason not to. Humans have commodified us, and the financial compensation for a natural bodily function is a no-brainer, especially once there's a mortgage to think about. Family men? Forget about it. How else would they be able to afford to take the kids to Blinxieland? May as well get paid for what's going down the shower drain every day."

Heat flooded her face at the image his carelessly spoken words presented: him, standing beneath a spray of water, muscular arm extended to brace himself against the wall with one hand, while the other gripped his straining erection, stroking himself until he came with a moan, painting the shower wall with a torrent of his copious release. He was wide enough to completely fill the shower in her small apartment, and there would be no room for her to join him for the activity unless she was impaled on his thick cock, legs wrapped around his waist. *Then there would be room, and he could give his arm a break. Wouldn't want him to get a cramp.*

"So just remember that," he went on, shaking her from her filthy daydream, "the next time a minotaur tries chatting you up, ask which facility he uses. If he swears up and down he's never been to a place like this, run away, because he's a liar."

Her laughter didn't travel around the room as freely now that she was ensconced beneath the bench, creaking once more with his weight above. Violet tried to envision herself flirting with another minotaur, another one of the clients from the farm perhaps or maybe some well-dressed stranger she might run into in Cambric Creek, visiting the farmer's market or in one of those odd little shops, but her imagination came up short, unable to picture any minotaur other than the messy-haired one above her. "Well, I can't say

I have many conversations with minotaurs outside of work, but I'll keep that in mind." From the bench above, he harrumphed and she laughed again. "I mean, it's not like there are minotaurs falling over themselves trying to buy me drinks when I'm out and about! But like I said—I'll keep it in mind. It's good to have a truth barometer. What do you mean this place is more selective?"

His hooves scraped on the footrests as he settled against the bench, and Violet depressed the pump bottle on her station, coating her palm with lubrication, her stomach flipping in anticipation.

"They have a health screening, and you have to meet certain criteria. Minimum height, minimum weight, they rate our production ability."

There was something strangely intimate about taking his huge cock in her hands now that they'd laughed together, she thought as he filled the opening. Like the last time, he was completely erect, hanging stiffly above like a particularly decadent, juicy-looking fruit. It was an unspoken expectation for the clients to already be partially aroused, speeding up the time they were in the chair and making things easier for the technician, and most clients followed the social courtesy. Walking in to find the minotaurs stroking themselves had lost its shock value for her at that point and she appreciated their efforts when she stood in position beneath the table, but this . . . this was a step beyond the normal courtesy. *Talking with you beforehand gets him hard. Very hard.* Violet understood the reaction, for she was certain if she were to take a seat on the vinyl-topped stool at that minute, a trail of moisture would betray her own arousal when she stood again.

"Production ability?" she asked, running the tips of her lubed fingers up the thickest of the snaking veins in his shaft, pausing to tease over the mid-length swell. He sucked in a sharp breath as she thumbed over the tip of his head, only a small crescent of the shiny skin exposed as his foreskin retracted, and she smiled, once again feeling a thrill at pulling a response from him. "How do they gauge that?"

"They measure our balls." His voice still retained its matter-of-fact edge, even as he breathed out raggedly, his cock bobbing as she released it, considering his words. His balls hung fat and full, impressive regardless of the species, and if there was some sort of test they were required to pass, Violet had no doubt that his would have outshone any they were judged against. "The bigger the testicles, the higher the rate of production, so they want to know that we're going to help them hit their acquisition targets."

He grunted when her hands raised to cup the testes in question, gliding her nails over each swell before tugging them gently, smiling when he shuddered. "And obviously you passed the test." She gave him another squeeze before moving back to his shaft, twisting her hands down to his head before she began to pump. His reply was lost to a choked groan as she stroked him, her entire upper body moving with her arms, the pretext of conversation forgotten for a moment as she lost herself in her task. "So are the other facilities similar in how they, um . . . operate?" She didn't like the prickle of jealousy that twisted her stomach at the thought of someone else milking him, stroking his girth and making him groan. He'd requested her, after all—he was *her* client. *Your big bull.* The rational part of her brain kicked at her spinal cord in an effort to wrestle back sense, but she ignored the shudder, settling into the rhythm she knew he liked.

"They don't have the same . . . personal touch this place does, and the personal touch is a definite perk."

"I guess it depends on who's doing the touching." The brazen flirtation was out before she could bite it back, but the answering chuckle—dark and deep, like a ripple of black velvet—made her sex quiver.

"There's no doubt about that. The ability to make requests is a perk of the perk, without question. Some personal touches are definitely more enjoyable."

It was all she could do to not climb the steps and flip him on the milking table and climbing aboard his broad body, straddling his hips and showing him just how *personal* her touch could be. Violet wondered if he could smell her arousal, for her panties had long since left behind damp and were making their best effort to achieve dripping. "I was surprised to have gotten a request at all, I think I'm the only human here and thought my hands were going to be too small for them to even keep me on. Glad to know the personal touch makes up for it. Is that why you put in the request in the first place?"

"Well, that and you do have those perfect, tiny little hands."

It was a relief being ensconced beneath the table, for he wasn't able to see her beaming smile or the way she bounced lightly on her toes, giddy with euphoria at the playful flirtation. "Just let me know if this personal touch is to your liking."

He grunted as she pulled his balls again with the hand not pumping his shaft, trying to stimulate every part of him to her best ability. *If a job's worth doing . . .*

"I can't think of a single way it could be any more to my liking," he gritted out through clenched teeth, trying and failing to hold in another growl of pleasure as she tightened her grip around his thick swell.

She imagined what it would be like to be stretched by his girth, her legs splayed over his hips as he bucked up into her, the way his big mushroom head would drag against her g-spot, her inner lips rubbed by that mid-shaft bulge; or else, how he might like for her to be on her knees before him, sucking on the seam of his sac as he stroked himself for her, feeling that pounding pulse in his balls against her mouth. She wondered if he would fall apart for her in the privacy of his own bed, his tight grunts and groans opening to full-throated moans of pleasure, if he would say filthy things to her in that rich, dark-chocolate voice as she writhed beneath him, stuffed with his thick cock, every pump of his wide hips sending her higher and higher up the cliff of her peak, threatening to fling her off the pinnacle into the sun once he came inside her, filling her with his heat . . .

His hips had begun steadily hitting the bench in that same slow, solid rhythm, making her realize how long it had been and how close she was to losing herself in her daydreams. She was eager for him to erupt, to see the proof of his big testicles' worth, a preposterous notion for her to be having, and the sensible part of her brain, which was shrinking by the week, stamped in disapproval. *We are going to have such a lecture when we get home tonight, young lady!*

When he released into the sucking nozzle once she'd worked it down his shaft, she quickly cupped his balls, feeling them pulse as they emptied in rhythmic spurts. She began pulling them, squeezing as she did so, milking them like udders, the way the Good Little Cows preferred, milking him dry.

He was unable to completely swallow down his groan of pleasure as she did so, jerking once, twice, sagging on the third, spent at last. The tension within her was so tight, a stiff breeze would have sent her over the edge, the merest ghost of pressure against her clit enough to make her come, and when the light clicked off, she nearly sobbed in need.

Her knees wobbled as she capped the bottle, weighing it and affixing the label, unhooking the used tank and hose. He'd not left the room yet, and she listened to the rustling sound of him silently redressing, turning at last to watch his broad back flex as he smoothed his re-tucked shirt, admiring the curve of his ass before he turned, dark brown eyes capturing her immediately. *Nothing about this is appropriate.*

"Where did you go for coffee?"

Her mouth ran dry, her jaw hanging open dumbly for several interminable moments before she was able to speak again, not expecting further conversation from the big bull.

"Um, there's a little plaza up the street, I don't even know what it was called. It's next to—"

"Next to the gym," he finished, making a sound of disgust at the back of his throat, his pink nose wrinkling around the burnished gold ring cinching it. Violet smiled at his reaction, following the ring as he shook his head. *He's just stupid handsome. If you ran into him on the street, you'd be following him home like a stray.* "That's terrible. You need to go to Black Sheep, they're over on Main with—"

"The one with the black awnings," she continued, nodding. "I've wanted to try it, but I never have time in the mornings and they always look so crowded when I pass on my way home."

He shrugged, his hand landing on the doorknob. "Find the time, you won't regret it. They roast their own beans on-site and age them in bourbon barrels, there's nothing better. I make a point of pulling away every afternoon for a caffeine fix. I expect a full review of your experience when you make it. Well . . . until next week."

She wasn't expecting the small smile—a brilliant flash of white teeth, his liquid brown eyes crinkling behind his untidy hair, leaving her utterly frozen—before he pulled the door open, horns ducking through to the hallway beyond, pulling it shut behind him. The collection room seemed to echo with his absence, the thud of her own heartbeat overloud without his bulk to absorb the evidence of what their sessions together did to her. Violet turned slowly, moving mechanically to complete her cleaning checklist before dragging her feet back to the locker room, collecting her little blue envelopes at the desk as she left.

* * *

She drove past the little coffee shop on Main Street without slowing; past the eclectic little shops and cafes until the signs for Bridgeton loomed ahead, leaving Cambric Creek behind for another day, her arousal forgotten as she entered her apartment, slumping into a chair. He looked younger when he smiled, she thought, less severe. She wondered what his laugh was like, if he shook with unrestrained mirth or if that too was tightly controlled, stifled like his pleasured moans. She wondered what she had done to earn the gift of his smile that day, what particular moment of their banter had he deemed charming enough to allow her a glimpse of that other, softer version of him she was certain existed. She was still sitting there when the room began to grow dim, the sunlight outside waning as the evening rolled in, but she had no desire to get up and start dinner, no desire to count the money from her collection of blue envelopes, already knowing what she'd find there.

She ought to get up and call her mother back, ought to video call them so she could talk to Aunt Gracie as well. She'd evade the truth or make something up, she'd already decided. They didn't need to know precisely what she was doing for a living, only that her bills were getting paid and she liked her co-workers. A pharmaceutical company had a nice panache to it, one that she knew would impress her mother and great aunt enough that there would be no need for further questions. *She'll probably go bragging back to Carson Tinsley's mom, letting her know how well I'm doing.* The thought of going for coffee with the human she'd known her whole life left her feeling oddly unsettled, imagining doughy-soft skin and middling height, exactly the same as every other guy she'd ever been with. *Tomorrow you're going to go to that little cafe in town for the good coffee, make the time, like he said.*

The thought did little to cheer her, and she slumped further into the corner of her chair. There was no real reason for her melancholy, she knew, no reason to mope. Her plan for solvency was coming together, her ability to catch up on her bills and begin paying down her debt becoming an attainable reality. She ought to be celebrating, ought to be continuing to revel in her reversal of fortune, despite the oddity of her new job. There was no reason for the bubble of despondency that had taken up residence in her chest; no reason she could think of other than one, and once the thought occurred to her, Violet knew it was true, a fact that boded poorly for the future.

It would be a whole week before she saw him again.

Chapter 6

T he Black Sheep Beanery was bustling as she stepped through the door the following afternoon, the smell of coffee reaching her before she'd even crossed the street. Violet felt a flare of nerves at being the only human in the room that she could see, feeling vulnerable without the protective coverings that her scrubs at the farm provided. Half of Cambric Creek seemed to be packed into the tight space: goblins and trolls and elves and gnolls, crowding around low tables and high tops, laughing over steaming paper cups as they pressed into armchairs, and standing at the long oak bar. She let out a ragged breath as she hesitantly joined the queue, half-wishing she'd stuck to the coffee shop in the little strip mall.

The sheep-faced man working the espresso machine never looked up from the line of labeled cups before him, his long dreadlocks gathered in a neat tie at the nape of his neck, swinging down his back as he efficiently added foamed milk to the tops of several of the cups before they were capped by an ivory-skinned elf who called out the names on the labels for the waiting patrons. Beside them, a tiefling with curling horns manned the cold drinks, shaking teas and iced lattes as if she were slinging high-end cocktails. She watched as a sleek-scaled lizard-woman claimed her cup once her name was called, barking into her cell phone the whole time, and Violet's eyes tracked her progress through the press of bodies, squeezing past a towering orc in a white lab coat and disappearing out the door.

The man in the queue ahead of her might have been human, she realized, studying his broad, well-muscled back, encased in a snug blue polo, tucked into uniform pants of the same color. The cashier was laughing at the conversation they had as she passed him his receipt, and as Violet watched, an employee from the backroom carried out two carafe boxes, passing them over the counter to the dark-haired man. *See? You're not the odd human out, it's fine. No one here even cares about that, probably.* When he turned, she had a smile ready, eager for the solidarity of shared species-hood, but there was something in the man's eye that made her shrink, her smile falling away. He was *ridiculously* handsome, his thick dark hair matched by his bittersweet chocolate eyes, a square jaw with a wide mouth, automatically turning up in a grin, a dimple appearing in his cheek . . . but the silver gleam in those dark eyes marked him as something other, more in common with the elves and goblins than her. His polo bore the emblem of the local firehouse, she saw, her eyes dropping, heat warming her cheeks as he nodded to her, the blinding white of his teeth obliterating everything else in the room.

"There's cream and sugar in the bag, Trapp!" the ewe-faced woman behind the counter said as he waved, the dreadlocked man behind the counter called out his own goodbye to the man before turning back to his espresso machine.

"What can we get for you today?"

Violet realized with a jolt that there was no one in front of her before the till, and that a smiling ewe-faced woman waited expectantly.

"Oh! Oh, um . . ." She'd been so wrapped up in watching the non-human residents, she had never glanced up to the menu, realizing too late that she had no idea what she wanted to order. The menu above was huge, she saw with a sinking heart, huge and unfamiliar, full of strange-sounding options that catered to the varied clientele. Her eyes zigzagged back and forth over menu items, absorbing none of it, her ability to read fleeing in her panic. Her brain seemed to freeze, grasping for something to blurt, her normal coffee order in the city, the mucky drink she'd tried at the little strip mall shop, anything at all that might break her muteness, but her mouth came up empty. *Just say something!* "I–um . . ."

"Is this your first time here?" the woman behind the counter asked kindly, perhaps intuiting that the human before her had completely lost her grasp of the common tongue, too wrapped up in gawking to even manage basic speech, smiling gently when Violet nodded with a flush. *Gee, is it that obvious?*

"The honeycomb latte is the most popular thing on our menu, that's what I'd recommend. It's our house espresso roast and the honeycomb comes from one of the local farms."

"Honey . . . that-that sounds perfect." She sagged in relief, face burning in mortification, thankful for the woman's patience. "I'll try that, thank you."

The little shop might need to be an only once-in-a-while luxury, she thought after swiping her card, the charge she just added to her bank card being pricier than even the chain near her apartment with the burnt coffee. The pick-up area was a press of bodies: small goblins and huge ogres, a graceful deer woman and a harpy with iridescent black feathers. The noise level was near deafening and Violet felt herself shrink, feeling awkward and out of place, wondering why she thought this was a good idea. She was going to find a corner to hide in, planned to grab her coffee and leave the moment her name was called . . . when an arm slipped through hers. A heady rush of perfume invaded her nostrils, bright white flowers and thick patchouli, the arm tugging her close with a determined strength, the clack and slide of several dozen bangles pressing into her forearm where she was gripped.

"Here you are, love! Come on, I got us a table already."

The girl's hair was bleached a silvery platinum blonde, spiky and shaved around her right ear, swinging long and silky past her left shoulder. Her piercing blue eyes were heavily lined in black with frosty white shadow, and they fixed on Violet with a heated intensity. She had no idea who this strange woman was, nor why she was acting like they were old acquaintances, but allowed herself to be pulled by the arm, too elated over not be the only human in attendance to care as the girl weaved through the packed pick-up area until they reached a tiny crescent of empty table, the spilled out contents of a well-worn black shoulder back holding it for their arrival. For the next seven minutes, she listened to the chattering woman tell an animated story about a man named Byron and his lack of common sense, his terrible sense of direction, and his inexplicable fear of water bears.

"I swear to fucking Dagda, I don't understand how anyone can be that thick after an extra hundred and forty years to sort themselves."

Violet nodded, utterly engrossed, despite not having any idea who Byron

65

was, who this woman was or why she was acting as if they were old friends, nor what an extra hundred and forty years even meant. Her name was called at that moment by the elf at the counter, her eyes darting to the steaming cup that had been placed at the pick-up station amid half a dozen others and back to her unlikely companion, uncertain if she was allowed to leave.

" 's'at you? Violet?" The girl stretched in her seat, craning her neck to see around a cluster of patrons at the bar, sagging in relief a moment later. "Perfect timing, that. He's gone. Would you be a luvvie and snag mine while you're up there? It's the lavender Earl Grey for Gilly."

Despite her earlier self-consciousness, Violet settled into her seat, the non-stop chatter and hum of the perpetually busy coffee shop settling into a pleasant white noise as she sipped her drink and listened to the girl. Her name was Geillis, and her pedestrian life as a university student had ended the night she was turned outside of a London concert hall in 1982. Violet had never met a vampire before, hadn't considered that vampires might be out and about in the middle of the day or drinking tea, had certainly never dreamt that she'd be shanghaied by one, but as she savored the velvety smoothness of her drink—the rich, malty coffee sweetened with a thick cutting of golden honeycomb and turned rich with cream—listening to to girl's heavily accented patter, she was incredibly grateful that she had been.

"Sorry 'bout all that waffle, thanks a ton for playing along, love. I hate running into folks from work outside the context, you know?"

She nodded again, pretending that she had any commensurate experience with that sort of thing, imagining the oddly-dressed vampire to be some sort of businesswoman, not wanting to make small talk with the boss on her off hours. "Did one of your co-workers come in?"

"Not strictly speaking, one of our donors. It's one thing to keep them entertained while you're draining them, quite another to have to suffer a chin wag on your own time. If that numpty-headed Byron had come in I'd have—"

"Donors?" Violet interrupted, unable to help herself, straightening in her seat. Her stomach flip-flopped at Geillis's words, trying to imagine making small talk with one of the Good Little Cows in the coffee line. "What-what do you mean donors? Draining them?"

"Right, at the restaurant. You ought to come by sometime, there's a side menu for you bleeders, so everyone is happy. The whole menu is *ethically sourced*, Ennis likes us to call it. The donors are screened every two weeks, no smoking, no drugs, clean eating for the duration of their contracts. About half of them are an easy go, just hook up the lines and have a chat. It's the other half you have to bloody worry over. Think the second the needle goes into their skin is the perfect time to have a wank. It's a fetish, being a feeder bleeder. Half the time they've got their pants open before I even get the tourniquet out."

Violet gaped. The girl was so matter-of-fact, so blasé about the tawdrier aspects of her apparent job, a job that sounded suspiciously similar to Violet's own. "Okay, wait . . . start over. Tell me everything."

La Vie Rouge was a vampire-centric restaurant in Cambric Creek's business district, she learned, catering to a fanged patronage, with a small menu of charcuterie boards and fruit plates for the regular clientele's "dinner guests." The proprietor, Ennis, had been a banker in his previous life; a respected member of his Victorian community with a wife and several children, before he'd been turned by a member of his church, a man with whom he'd had several sexual dalliances. Geillis told the story in a hushed voice, leaning over her cup of tea with bright, expressive eyes, and Violet was certain she could smell the petrichor from the rainy night she described, could see the steam rising off the pavement beneath the yellow glow of gas lamps as the man was bitten during a clandestine, back-alley assignation. The numpty-headed Byron was his partner, clinically inept and a disgrace to vampires everywhere, according to Geillis.

"I'm telling you, he must be bloody fucking brilliant in bed, tha's the only reason I can think of for Ennis to have decided 'wotcher, I've the whole world to pick from, but this gormless muppet is me true love.' It's the only explanation."

"And you take the blood from the menu donors?" Violet went on, undeterred, a bubble of giddiness rising within her, "and sometimes they're *jerking off*?!"

The two goblins at the adjacent table paused their conversation to glance up at her enthusiastic exclamation, as an orc at the table across from theirs raised a thick, dark eyebrow, a smile tugging at the corner of his full lips around his tusks. Heat burned up her neck, but she was too excited to be mortified. *She has a job just like yours!* Before the vampire could even respond, Violet was continuing, overwhelmed with the need to get it all out, to tell someone, to tell her everything.

"I work at Morning Glory Milking Farm, have you heard of it? I–we milk minotaurs. That's–that's my job. I'm a milking technician."

Geillis's mouth formed a perfect 'o' of surprise for several beats before her darkly-lined lips broke into a wolfish smile, showing off her pointed canines. "Minotaurs don't have udders, not that I'm aware of . . . so what exactly is it you're milking?" Violet didn't need to answer, for the other girl had already dissolved into laughter, her platinum head dropping to the table.

"Well, that's the best gig in town, innit? You at least get to work with big, beefy minotaurs. I'm stuck with humans! Mmmm, I'll bet that's some prime beef you get to manhandle . . ."

"Grade A certified," she giggled, elation wiping out the previous afternoon's melancholy. "Can you believe that's a job?! Although, I would never have guessed being a literal menu item was a job either. I love it here, it's just . . . it's so different from everything I'm used to! The job pays really well, so I have no complaints."

"Cheers to that," the smiling vampire said, raising her paper cup. "This town is full of some odd ducks, but it's nice having neighbors who aren't rounding up pitchforks over every little thing. I can complain about Byron until Crackadam, but Ennis and the restaurant . . . it's a good place to be. Promise you'll come by some time!"

Violet tapped her nearly empty cup against the side of the other girls', beaming. She *did* want to visit the vampire restaurant, wanted to get a glimpse of the infamous Byron and learn what sorts of dishes were on the menu for the vampire clientele. She wanted to see what that intriguing little shop was with the stained glass windows and learn what a talon dip entailed at the nail salon; wanted to explore all of the interesting corners of Cambric Creek—which to her, would be all of it. There was nothing like this back home in her human neighborhood, nothing like this eclectic little coffee shop, catering to all of the different members of the community, and she'd certainly never have the chance to befriend a vampire if she were sitting there making stilted conversation with Carson Tinsley from up the street. She was glad she'd met Geillis, glad she'd made the time to come, Violet decided. *He was right. It was worth it.*

III

Part Three

Chapter 7

"Mmmm, just like that, right there . . . that's what I like. Don't stop now, sugar, you keep that up."

She grimaced from her place beneath the breeding bench, glancing down to the digital clock on the table. She'd worked on this bull before and heard stories from the other collection techs—he wasn't quite one of the Good Little Cows, didn't need the fantasy of being milked like an actual dairy heifer, but it was clear he was there for the hand job. Violet was half convinced he'd not notice if his bottle was never scanned in, no payment routing to his account. He came for the sexual release, and didn't let the associate under the bench forget it.

She nearly lost her grip as the minotaur above shifted, repositioning himself to be able to thrust harder against the hole in the bench. She had no doubt that he was likely a terrible lover, if the sharp, erratic bobs of his cock were any indication. *Being on the receiving end of that would be like getting a root canal for your vagina.*

"Squeeze my balls with your other hand, but keep that up now . . . mmm, perfect. You're gonna have me cumming so hard."

The timer on the table rolled over to the fifteen-minute mark, which was good enough for her. Reaching back, she flipped on the machine one-handed and took up the nozzle. If he wanted to talk about ejaculating, there was no time like the present. The minotaur jerked when she applied the nozzle, his protest turning to a groan as the sucking silicone worked down his shaft, and she peeled off the oil-coated gloves, readying the label. She'd been working at the farm for several months at that point, and while clients like this might have fazed her in the beginning, they did so no longer.

"There we go," she agreed as the green light clicked on. She'd not be earning a tip from this particular bull now, but then again, she likely wouldn't have anyway. *Get them in and out and on with their day.* There was a Good Little Cow in her rotation that afternoon bookended with Earners, and she only hoped the afternoon would pass quickly. A purple sticker loomed on the bottom of her stack of files, and thus every hour before the one that signified her last appointment of the day was merely to be endured.

* * *

He visited the farm on Fridays and had confided that he liked to do so because he often traveled for work on the weekends. She had no idea what line of work he was in nor what his travel entailed, and if she were being completely honest with herself, his confidence had been more of a matter-of-fact declaration and she'd needed to suppress the urge to snap to attention with a notebook, taking dictation as he towered above her. That hadn't stopped her from using the small bits of information she gleaned to pad her daydreams with solidity, each tiny nugget adding to the shape of him in her mind.

The information on his chart was minimal. He weighed almost as much as her compact car and was more than a decade her senior. Violet pondered if he would find her too young to be a viable romantic partner; if their disparate social positions would be a turn-off. *After all, he's obviously successful. Three months ago you had to buy gas station coffee and generic orange juice.* She'd been sipping her juice before her laptop when the thought had occurred to her, scowling at the voice in her head. She *still* bought the generic orange juice, but now she did it because she found she preferred the taste, she rationalized.

She wasn't out of the woods yet, not by a long shot, but for the first time since she'd been out on her own, her bank account had a four-digit balance. She'd been able to set her credit card bills to auto-pay, a luxury reserved for only those who always knew where their next dollar was coming from and didn't need to stress over having money for basic necessities. She was still in debt and drinking generic juice, nowhere on his lofty level, but she was holding her own. And besides, she reminded herself peevishly, she was well educated and highly motivated, and she only needed the right opportunity to come along before her own career would be underway.

She wondered if he worked in one of the nearby industrial parks, as he'd mentioned coming to his appointments with her from work, and she'd deduced from their previous conversations that he obviously lived in Cambric Creek. He'd once lived in Bridgeton, but he'd clearly stated that he *used* to live in the city. She wondered where he'd called home then, if he'd lived in one of the expensive high rises around the downtown area or something more akin to her own dilapidated little building, full of pensioners and cash-strapped students. She'd looked up Starling Heights next, discovering it was another town, separated from Cambric Creek by Greenbridge Glen, a tiny resort community nestled in rolling, green hills. He didn't live in the resort town, of that she was certain, and he'd complained about the distance to Starling Heights, which made Cambric Creek the most likely option.

She'd detoured off the main road on her way home one afternoon, turning down streets until she found herself in the residential section of town, housing development after housing development of tidy properties. The architecture had enough variation to keep the streets from looking identical, but there was clearly a city planning commission and she wondered what the homeowners association fees must be.

The second time she'd eschewed her direct route home, Violet noticed a theme. There wasn't simply a difference in the generic architecture of the homes. There were distinctly different builds that boasted the same features, repeated over and over: the houses with extra-wide, paved driveways also had outsized doorways, while other houses had no drive to speak of, just a wide expanse of green lawn and visible water features. Single-level dwellings that boasted no front steps sat beside more traditional-looking houses with extremely small doors; some yards boasted thick, lush grass, and others were partially covered with sand. The coffee shop wasn't the only aspect of the town that catered to its varied residents, clearly. She tried to imagine what sort of house he lived in; if the residents moved into homes based on their species or had things custom-tailored after the fact. Beyond the endless streets of developments was a gated road bearing elvish lettering she was unable to read, the homes contained within sitting beyond an artificial slope, protecting them from looky-loos like her.

Her return drive took her through a neighborhood called Oldetowne, as evidenced by the ornate placards on either side of the intersection, and true to its name, the streets were lined with stately Victorians and palatial edifices that looked like something out of a movie set in the roaring twenties, and she'd been breathless with excitement over such a find, feeling her pulse race for reasons that had nothing to do with the corresponding beat between her thighs, for the first time in weeks.

Her art history degree had funneled into a specific discipline—western architecture of the previous two centuries and the ornamental hallmarks of the different styles. Her master's degree in non-profit management had meant to be the finishing block on a staircase to her dream job, and to be surrounded by such a bounty . . . she would have gladly given her left foot to get a look inside one of the pristine houses lining the street.

She'd pulled to the curb in wonder, trying and failing to imagine what sort of residents lived there, unable to picture her minotaur calling one of these Queen Annes home; he seemed a touch too rugged for that, even with his well-pressed shirts. She'd not run into him wandering the streets of Cambric Creek, but the different neighborhoods fueled her fantasies all the same.

According to his chart at the farm, he'd been born in the dead of winter, mid-January, when the temperatures were coldest and the snow piled high. She'd never put much stock into horoscopes before, but now found herself curled up in bed at night with her tablet, reading about the responsible, serious natures possessed by Capricorns. Distant and driven, with a healthy respect for material security and a tremendous libido . . . Violet didn't pretend to know the first thing about astrology, but she was forced to admit the description seemed accurate, at least from what she could tell with her limited knowledge base. She'd never given much thought to her own sun sign, but the fact that her spring birthday was represented by a bull thrilled her, and she poured over new age websites reading about their sexual and emotional compatibility and chances for relationship success. She wondered if other species read horoscopes, or if it was a uniquely human distraction, deciding she'd ask Geillis. She had no doubt that his sober, stern nature meant he would scoff at her ditherings, but it warmed her knowing that their compatibility was written in the stars.

She had it bad.

She'd tried her hardest to avoid it, to prevent it from happening, had even considered that she *should* go home for a weekend and have coffee with Carson Tinsley from up the street, but there was no way around it. She had a ridiculous crush on the messy-haired minotaur, and every week spent in his gruff company pulled her further down, unable to think of anything but him, going over every conversation they'd had over the past few months in an effort to root out the most innocuous details she might have overlooked.

* * *

"Violet, I have good news and bad news," called Donnaxa, the cheerful beetle-woman who handled the files with Magda, appearing at the top of the hallway as she exited the collection room. In an instant, her heart seemed to climb to her throat, thoughts of her ridiculous crush replaced with the very real fear of being fired. *Violet, we know about your inappropriate fantasies. The janitorial staff has notified us of the snail trail left behind on your workbench. Please collect your things.*

"What do you want to hear first?"

"Um, the bad, I guess?" she squeaked out, hoping her knees would continue to hold her. *This is it, this is the end. No more delicious coffee and being friends with vampires. You're gonna need to move home. You'll have to marry Carson Tinsely and move into his mom's basement and take vacations in the loft above the garage.*

"Well, the bad news is your next appointment canceled, he called about an hour ago."

She had curled in on herself—anticipating the blow of being told to collect her things, to leave immediately—and her eyes had scrunched tight, her hands gripping the stack of files with white knuckles. At Donnaxa's words, her eyes creaked open. Canceled. A canceled client. *That's it, you're not fired, it's just a cancellation. What's wrong with you, how would they even know?!*

"O-oh! Okay, well . . . that's not terrible. What's the good news?"

"The good news is that the client after that canceled as well, and he was the one who requested the milkmaid scrubs."

The beetle-woman beamed and Violet sagged in relief, letting out a shaky laugh. It didn't matter that the Good Little Cows were usually excellent tippers, *not* having to deal with one was a boon for which she was grateful. "Oh, I'm just crushed. Guess that means a long lunch then? Should I go clock out?"

"Yes, please! Go enjoy yourself, you've earned it!"

Geillis started her shifts at La Vie Rouge in the mid-afternoons, draining the day's menu donors early enough that their blood had time to congeal and be turned into dramatic culinary offerings: decorative aspics and foams, artfully plated on spotless white dinnerware. She'd poured over the restaurant's website and menu, marveling over the fanciness and ingenuity of the dishes, despite each only consisting of a single ingredient, desperately wanting to try it and not brave enough to go on her own. The gift of a free afternoon was not one she'd likely get again anytime soon, and if she texted Geillis now, they might at least have time to meet for coffee.

Perfect, I'm just up the street at the bank. I'll get us a table

The time to get coffee with her friend, get a bit of fresh air, and she'd still come back to the farm to see him for her final slot of the afternoon. It was, Violet thought, waving to the cheerful goblin at reception, a perfect day.

Chapter 8

She'd not yet visited the Black Sheep Beanery when it wasn't crowded with bodies, and was beginning to suspect the coffee house was packed with customers from the moment it opened at sunrise until the point they needed to physically evict the stragglers in the evenings.

It had become a game for her, listening to the conversations of the different species that crowded together as a community within the confines of the small shop and eavesdropping on their orders, learning which menu items were geared to the particular clients.

"A medium chlorophyll chiller, a kid's size malted moss sweetsteam, and—Finny, what kind of lolly do you want?"

The tiefling behind the counter sighed as the small, amphibious child pressed his webbed hands to the glass to ogle the confections within the case, leaving behind twinned smudges behind. Violet grinned as the child announced his selection, his mother groaning, correcting him that one of the elaborate desserts hadn't been an option. She wondered what sort of child a human and minotaur would have together, trying to imagine a baby with messy hair and velvety-soft ears, and a slender, swishing tail. *Okay, literally what is even wrong with you. Your ovaries need to get a fucking grip. You don't want kids for at least a decade, if ever.* She was forced to concede that the voice in her head was right, as she watched the child smear his small, blue tongue over the glass in front of the cake he wanted, as though he might be able to taste it through the case, and the cashier sighed heavily once more. *A decade at least.*

There was a tantruming toddler somewhere near the door behind her,

80

as well as what sounded like a cluster of adolescents off to the side of the line, giggling and squealing noisily, and she reflected that teens were teens, regardless of species.

"Tell them it doesn't matter what their suppliers are saying. Their suppliers are lying. Are we really supposed to believe there's not a single axle available to ship on the whole eastern seaboard? They need to figure it out and make the client happy, end of story. Mhm, that's it. Check-in when your plane lands, alright?"

Her stomach flip-flopped at the familiar edge, the deep, demanding tone . . . *see, look what you've gone and done. Start thinking about babies that you don't actually want to have and now your ovaries are imagining they hear him everywhere.* Her phone buzzed then, a text from Geillis. *Just grabbed a table, near the windows.*

"What can we get for you today?" The horned cashier was addressing her, she realized, only just noticing that the little frog-like boy and his mother had finally moved on. "The honeycomb latte, please. Medium." Violet had no doubt that there were other delicious offerings on the menu, but she was a creature of habit and the decadent, honey-drenched latte was too good not to order.

"And name for the order?"

She could feel the heat from the patron in line behind her as she gave the cashier her name, suddenly stepping forward, close enough that if she were to step backward, she'd be trodding over their toes, a discomfiting closeness. The tiefling nodded, opening her mouth to speak when her eyes raised, her attention caught by something over Violet's head, her lips quirking up in a half-smile, before nodding.

"A large red eye—cream, no sugar, and whatever floofy dessert drink she's ordering . . . and maybe one of the caramel pecan twists."

She stiffened when the unseen too-close patron spoke, realizing her ovaries hadn't been imagining things, his deep, resonant voice just as decisive and firm as it was when it rang across the milking room floor. Violet felt her insides turn to jelly at the sound of it, the sound of *him*, her knees joining suit a moment later when a huge, warm hand landed on the center of her back, gently moving her aside to take her place before the register, swiping his card and completing the transaction for her coffee before she had the wherewithal to do anything more than gape up at him.

"Oh, *maybe* one of the twists," the familiar ewe-faced woman laughed from her place behind the counter, shaking her head as she placed a gooey-looking pastry in a small paper bag, passing it to the big minotaur with the messy hair, the light overhead catching on the gold ring that spanned across his wide, pink nose. "You're going to turn into one of these twists."

He huffed—a familiar, *delicious* sound that went to that place between her thighs she'd dreamed of him licking, a fantasy that spurred suppositions over how rough his tongue was, if it would be velvety smooth or textured and coarse; if he'd press it into her and lick her clit until she came against its unknown texture, flooding his mouth with her own honey. In this particular daydream, the taste of her would drive him him crazy, his thick cock would already be drooling pre-come in anticipation, and he would flip her before the tremors of her orgasm would even be over, unable to control his ardor for another minute. He would enter her from behind and make her clench around his girth as he pumped into her with those slow, solid thrusts, his heavy balls slapping her still-trembling clit, making her come again around his cock.

Violet was certain she was about to swoon, the lights overhead suddenly too bright and the voices of the other patrons too loud, her thoughts too obscene for the polite company of the little coffee shop.

"Fancy meeting you here." His voice was a rumble of thunder caught in the mountains, the deep and sonorous warning of a coming storm, and as her eyes darted around wildly—taking in his perfectly tailored dress pants ending in a neat tuck above his jutting hocks, his polished, ebony hooves with no scuff in sight and far larger than she'd anticipated—Violet wanted to be caught in his downpour, wanted to be *drenched* by him. "I suppose this means you can't say minotaurs aren't buying you drinks when you're out and about."

"No, I suppose I can't," she murmured, face heating. She felt the weight of his eyes moving over her, slowly and deliberately, completely unlike her own frenzied observance, realizing this was the first time he was seeing her out of the farm's uniform scrubs. She wished she had taken a bit longer on her hair that morning, that she'd managed more than just a swipe of mascara before she'd raced out the door. *At least you're wearing decent clothes today and not just leggings and a crop top.* She had decided weeks earlier that one of her favorite things about working at the farm was the provided uniform, leaving her free to dress as comfortably as she wanted for her drive. In truth, the clothes she had on that day were 100% nicer than what she normally wore to work, on account of having avoided laundry for the last two weeks. She watched his eyes travel the short distance up her unremarkable frame before they finally made their way to hers, and she was unable to read the charged expression in them. *He probably doesn't even like humans.* "You-you didn't need to do that, you know."

He'd not removed his hand until the bag had been passed across the counter, and she still felt the phantom weight of it, heavy and warm on the small of her back, exactly the way it was in all of her fantasies. "Of course I didn't," he agreed in that low, firm voice, eyes still locked on hers, "but I wanted to."

"Rourke, are you and Lurielle coming to my Irus Day cookout?"

The moment was broken when his head raised in response to the sheep-woman's voice, and Violet realized with a jolt that the question had been directed at him. *Rourke.* The initials on his file had been the most intriguing question mark of all, *R M* followed by the eight-digit identification number. She had poured over non-human baby-naming websites, looking up the most common minotaur names of the last several decades, trying to decide if he seemed like a Rhugar or a Ravis. *Rourke.* It was simple and crisp, and suited him perfectly. Violet couldn't wait until she was alone, to say his name aloud and learn its shape, tasting it on her tongue, feeling enormously grateful to the caprine barista for the windfall of information. *Wait . . . what did she say? Who's Lurielle?*

"As long as I'm in town, I'll pop in. You know I can't make any promises with my schedule."

She tsked, shaking her head at his non-committal response. "We haven't seen the two of you in months. I'm not taking no for an answer."

"Well, if I'm traveling, you can put a picture of my head on a popsicle stick and pretend I'm there. I'm not making plans for Lurielle, don't try to get me in trouble like that."

Violet's warm feelings for the ewe-faced woman shriveled as she continued to good-naturedly carp over Rourke and the mysterious Lurielle having missed the last several parties she'd thrown. Of course he wasn't single. Of course there was a girlfriend in the picture, maybe even a wife, she realized with a sinking stomach. Somehow, in all of her daydreams, she'd never imagined him being coupled, even though she should have suspected he would be. Handsome, successful, a voice that sent a shiver up the listener's back and a cock that would leave his partner seeing stars . . . expecting that he'd be single to boot was a fanciful bit of wishful thinking on her part. It was foolish and naive to assume that visiting the farm meant he was single, to assume he hadn't been including himself in the description of family men with a mortgage and kids at home, with a fashionable, svelte businesswoman for a wife. It was patently idiotic to assume he'd ever be interested in someone like her: an unremarkable human, no career, drowning in debt, nothing to bring to the table with someone like him.

Suddenly, there was nowhere she wanted to be less than standing at his side, listening to him make fun weekend plans with the barista and his apparent wife or girlfriend. Geillis was waiting for her, after all. *This is what you get for taking your eye off the ball, this job is supposed to get you out of debt and help tide you over until you find something real.* She could change her schedule, would pick up a weekend shift and ensure that she no longer worked on Fridays, would put him out of mind and forget her silly, one-sided crush. His hooves barely made a sound as he edged around the counter, and she realized for the first time that the dark wood was actually some sort of laminate, spongy enough to absorb the heavy tread of sharp hooves and thundering orcs alike. *You'll probably never be coming back here, so why does it matter.* The voice in her head was right about that—this place would be forever tainted now.

"You're not going home early, are you?"

As ever, his question had a ring of demand, trapping her in his pointed gaze. Violet swallowed down her emotion and squared her shoulders. She had been a fool, but she didn't need to continue acting like one. "I had a cancellation," she explained, using her overly sunny customer service voice. A small furrow appeared between his eyes, velvety soft and slightly vexed, and she had to clench the soft leather of her clutch to keep from stretching up on her toes to smooth it away. *No more of that. You're done being stupid over him.*

"Chlorophyll chiller for Sleeva, honeycomb latte for Violet, and a red eye for Rourke."

His big hand reached out, palming her latte before she could turn towards the pickup counter. "Violet."

The sound of her name uttered in his rich, deep voice was enough to rock her off her tentative foundation of determination. Her name in his voice invoked a field of her namesake flower, rich and lush and purple, more sensuous than she could ever remember it being said, and she forced herself to swallow down her disappointment. *Stupid, so stupid.* "Thanks again for that, you really didn't need to . . ." His hands hadn't fully relinquished control of the steaming cup, even though her small fingers had already curled around the heat guard, and the brush of his skin, so soft and warm, made her quiver.

He hummed, a deep vibration of air she felt in her own lungs, unable to force her pinky—the same one that had slipped into his foreskin, caressing his cockhead from within, making him groan in pleasure—away from where it pressed against his thick fingers, unsure if the heat she felt came from the hot cup of coffee or from his skin.

"Like I said, I wanted to. Would you care to—"

"Well, there's someone waiting for me, so I should let you get back to work." The words came out in a tumble, not realizing she'd spoken over him until they were already out, unsure of what he'd been saying. The cup was relinquished fully, surrendered to her waiting hand, although he did not back away.

"Lunch date?"

There was an edge to the thunderclap, and his eyes seemed to bore into hers, holding her captive in their chocolate depths. *What difference does it make to him?* she thought, jutting out her chin defiantly. "Exactly."

Neither of them had moved a muscle, but it suddenly seemed as if a lake of distance separated them, the warmth in his eyes shuttering, pushing her out to stand on a far-off shore. "Then I ought not keep you." He straightened, his posture seeming a fraction tighter than it had only a moment before. "Until this afternoon . . . Violet."

She had no idea how she managed to prevent her knees from buckling as she wove through the bodies, feeling the heavy weight of his eyes on her back until she turned the corner, heading to the side wall. Geillis sat with her untouched Earl Grey steaming before her, her mouth slightly open as she gaped. "Who was *that?*"

"W-what?"

"Don't what me like a fish, who was that *delicious* slab of beef?"

The realization that her friend had seen her talking to him, to Rourke, made her cheeks heat again. *So much for this being a perfect day.* "Just a client," she grumbled, glaring down at the latte, still feeling the phantom brush of his fingers against her own. "No one important."

The vampire laughed incredulously, shaking her bleached head. "luvvie, come off it. That was *not* 'just a client.' I was coming out of the loo while you were standing there mooning at each other like it was a private suite."

Violet glared at her friend's knowing smirk and laughing eyes. "What were you doing in the bathroom?" she demanded, attempting to turn the conversation around. "Do vampires even *need* to use the bathroom?"

"No, uh uh, that's not going to work. We can discuss the intricacies of the vampiristic lifestyle and the maintenance and upkeep of an asymmetrical haircut another time. I want to hear about that big, sexy friend of yours. He quite gave me the shivers! Looks like the type that might enjoy taking you over his knee if you've been a naughty girl, if you know what I mean."

The image Geillis's words put in her head—one of her, wearing her best interview outfit, the slim-fitting pencil skirt down around her ankles along with her panties, the red outline of his hand stinging her still-jiggling ass cheek as she splayed over his knees; the solid, steel shape of his erection pressing through his perfectly tailored trousers—made her drop her head to the table with an audible thunk, squeezing her eyes shut and wishing she had just stayed home today. *You should call the office and tell Donnaxa you're feeling sick. It's only him and two other clients you'd be missing, and then tomorrow put in an availability change.*

"He's not anyone," she insisted from the crook of her elbow, still feeling the weight of his hand at her back. *Rourke.* "He's no one important."

"Mhmm. Methinks the lady doth protest a bit too bloody much, but we'll let it slide . . . for now. I can promise you he won't be 'nobody' for long."

Chapter 9

The thought of leaving the other collection technicians in a lurch had her returning to the farm, despite her heart wanting to hide away to lick its wounds, and soon she was finishing off her first Earner of the afternoon, listening to his Bluetooth conversation as he dressed and she scanned in his bottle.

"Maybe you can talk some sense into him. Jannith, I'm just saying—the second that ring goes in, that's it, it's all over. They can still do the whole ceremony and vows thing, and if it's not a huge fucking mistake, he can get the ring put in for their anniversary. He's your brother, you need to talk to him. It's not too late to back out."

The last client's voice trailed as he exited the upper portion of the collection room, leaving her alone. She had wondered about the ring he—*Rourke*—wore in his nose. The accouterment was sported by many of the minotaurs who visited the farm, and she'd assumed it was for cultural reasons, like the intricate braids worn by orcs, but it had seemed insensitive to question. *It's fine, it's going to be fine. He's a client, and you can make small talk with him like a normal client today, and put in for an availability change first thing tomorrow.*

She half-expected him to still be gripping the same coffee cup as she entered the room. The same furrow rested between his eyes, tightening his features, and she pushed her heart back down her throat. *You can do this.*

"Long time no see!" she called out cheerfully in the same, cheery customer service voice she'd used earlier. His mouth pressed in a firm, flat line, his eyes tracking her movement around the lower portion of the room.

"I have a cultural question for you," she said, deliberately turning away to pull a tank from the rack. *Make small talk, don't talk about this afternoon.* "If it's not disrespectful to ask. What does the ring in the nose signify? I've always wondered, and the client before you was talking on the phone about convincing someone not to do it. Is it a religious thing?"

He stiffened, the weight of that afternoon and that great gulf of distance still sitting between them. For a weighted moment, he said nothing, his hands unbuckling his belt in slow motion. When he spoke at last, his voice was low and clipped. "Historically, it's a symbol of ownership, being bound to another. The modern usage is almost always to signify being bound to another in marriage."

She nodded, her suppositions confirmed. *Don't cry, there's nothing to cry over. Maybe you can change your availability on the portal as soon as you get home.* The thought that this might be the last time she saw him—the last time she would talk with him and flirt with him, the last time she would hold his heavy cock, the last time she might see that transforming smile that made him seem so much softer—made her throat stick, and she quickly moved beneath the table to shuffle papers on her clipboard. Although, he'd not yet smiled at her, hadn't given any indication that he was going to do anything more than glower from the top of the room, and in all likelihood, the last time for all the things she would miss was probably last week.

"I've been divorced for about two years now . . . just haven't had the damned thing taken out. At first, I wasn't ready, now I'm afraid it's going to hurt."

The air in her lungs seemed to freeze, the blood in her veins slowing to a halt, leaving her suspended and immobile beneath the bench. *Divorced?* It took a moment for her brain to force her to breathe once more, culling the brief flare of hope. *So he's divorced, so what. She's a girlfriend then.* "Well, I'm sure getting it removed couldn't possibly be more painful than having it put in in the first place," she forced out, in that same high-pitched, too-chipper voice. *That doesn't change anything.*

"How was your lunch date?"

His words were a sharp bark, tinged with something else she couldn't immediately define; a question to which he demanded an answer. He'd straddled the bench by then but had made no move lean forward, and Violet had the feeling he'd keep her waiting indefinitely until she responded. "It was very nice, I haven't been able to do anything in the afternoon like that in months. Thanks again for the coffee. So . . . sounds like you've got some fun weekend plans coming up?" She didn't know what possessed her to continue the line of questioning, playing this tense little tit-for-tat game with him, but the question escaped her traitorous mouth, matching his sharp, accusatory tone before she could suck it back in. *What happened to meaningless small talk?!*

"Xenna lives in the same development. She and her brother Xavier—the ram with the dreads? They own the coffee house together, did you know that? She and her husband love throwing big block parties . . . it's always a little claustrophobic for my tastes, but I try to pop in when I can. Now she wants us to RSVP, which is asking a bit too much."

"Who's Lurielle?

There was no way her tone could be construed as anything *but* antagonistic, and fire engulfed her the instant she'd spat the question out, mortification burning her alive, and she only hoped it would put her out of her misery swiftly. Silence seemed to fill the space like a tangible cloud. Violet wondered if she'd be able to back out of the room without earning his notice, if she crept like a mouse, backing towards the door, she might be able to wrench it open and flee before he could twist on the bench to catch her exit.

"Lurielle is my neighbor."

The words came out in a low growl tinged with frustration, and she was forced to reach out for the table to hold herself up. *His . . . neighbor? Not a wife or a girlfriend. The fucking neighbor?!*

"She lives next door. She's an elf . . . an elf with a huge orc boyfriend. We used to go to all these block parties together because we were the only singles at the time. Not anymore, obviously."

"Oh," she whispered, shrinking beneath the table. *His neighbor. He was going to ask you to have coffee with him, you could have made out in the parking lot, but instead you pretended to have a date and she's his fucking neighbor.* The room blurred, the tears she'd been holding in for the previous several hours unable to be dammed up for another moment. The way he'd darkened when she'd said she was meeting someone, all of the warmth going out of him . . . *Your Capricorn lover will be prone to fits of jealousy and possessiveness. Piquing his jealousy is a good way to remind him to treasure his mate, as long as his feeling of security in the relationship is quickly assuaged.*

"My friend Geillis, that's who I had coffee with today. I met her last month at the coffee shop, she kidnapped me to keep from talking to one of her clients at work, and we've been friends since." An interminable pause followed her disclosure, with no hint of movement from above.

"*That's* who you were meeting?"

Violet could hear the scowl in his voice, and a quick glance upwards showed her the way his hands curled tightly around the side of the bench. "Yes," she squeaked. "She-she works at La Vie Rouge, it's a vampire restaurant in the business district?"

"I know of it. She's a vampire?"

"Mhm. I really want to go there, just to see what it's like . . . there's nothing like that where I'm from. I grew up in an all-human town, did I ever tell you that? Anyway . . . that's who I was meeting today."

The shadow of his horns on the ground beside her shifted as her rambling cut off, as if he were shaking his head. "Do vampires even drink coffee?"

"She orders tea," Violet laughed hoarsely, rubbing away the foolish evidence of her tears, listening to the bench creak overhead as he shifted, those huge, polished hooves scraping against the footrest as he settled into place at last. "And she doesn't drink it. She just holds it and smells it. Says it helps her remember."

"And you're not afraid of being in a restaurant with all those hungry vampires?"

"No!" she exclaimed, her laughter buffeted by his big body, filling the hole in the table and sealing out the light. The shift in the conversation was baffling, the levity in both their voices, as if the enormous weight that had rested over the room when she'd entered had been plucked away, and she bounced on her toes giddily. *He was single!* She tried to remind herself that nothing had changed, he was still a client and she was still just his milking technician, but a weightless euphoria surged through her all the same. "I think it's fascinating.

91

Like I said, I'm from a human town originally, so I didn't grow up with other species the way people around here are. I really love it though, when my lease is up I'm thinking of maybe trying to find something in the area to eliminate the drive. So . . . an elf and an orc live next door to you?"

"Not quite, just the elf. Her boyfriend lives in Bridgeport. He comes to my gym when he stays with her on weekends, and he lifts an *absurd* amount of weight. I'm waiting for him to pull something in his groin or pop a blood vessel in his eye, it's only a matter of time before it happens."

She laughed, imagining the posturing that must go on at a multi-species gym. "You should probably offer to spot him, I'm sure she would appreciate that." His cock swayed, full and fat, thickened with arousal and waiting for her, and he chuckled as she lubed up her hands. "I'll bet he would have already had a ring taken out of his nose, too. Orcs are super tough, right?" He harrumphed at that and she smiled, wishing she could lean up and place a soft kiss to the shiny-pink crescent of that domed helmet, just barely peeking out from its fleshy confines. *If there wasn't a camera, you'd suck out his soul.*

"I'm not so sure about that. They put rings on their tusks, that's like piercing a fingernail. There are no nerve endings involved . . . I grew up on the edge of a human town, sort of in-between their town and our settlement. My grandmother was human, so it never felt like an awkward thing, not until I was older. No vampire restaurants there either."

The confidence seemed like a precious gift, one that she would add to the shape of him in her head, solidifying him further. *Make your Capricorn mate feel valued and appreciated and he'll make you the center of his world.* Rourke let out a ragged breath as she gripped him—stroking him slowly, reverently, *lovingly*, trying to channel her feelings through the tips of her fingers—and chuckled again, relaxing fully against the bench as he hardened in her hands.

"So . . . the ring out and a vampire restaurant. We'll have to see what we can do about that."

IV

Part Four

Chapter 10

"I'm gonna come," the spotted bull moaned, bellowing as his horns cut through the air. "I'm gonna come so hard for you . . ."

"You're the best breeding bull in the stable," Violet assured the minotaur above her "I'm going to milk you dry."

The Good Little Cows were, if nothing else, a predictable lot. The bucked and bellowed, stamping and scraping their hooves against the stocks as if they were about to charge, begging to be milked like the cows they were. Of all the things she'd learned about minotaurs in the several months she'd been at the farm, this particular kink was the most eye-opening. She'd begun to wonder, as she moved amongst the different species of employees at the farm and the residents of Cambric Creek, if they *all* possessed different species-specific sexual proclivities.

She recalled a conversation with Geillis, in which the vampire had pointed out the obvious human kink Violet had been ignorant of before taking this job.

"It's interesting, innit?" the vampire had reflected, inhaling the fragrant steam from her cup. "There're a fair bit of you bleeders here in town, but it's all women. You know what that means, right?" She'd had no clue, and Geillis had rolled her eyes. "You're all just a bit curious, just a little inquisitive . . . come to a new place, try food you've never heard of . . . and then you find out that naga who sold you insurance last week has two cocks, and *obviously* you're curious about that as well. So then you ride one of those cocks, just to see what it's like, of course. And then take a turn on the other. And then he slips 'em both in, and there's no human with one boring little cock who will ever be good enough again after that, not now that you've been dp'ed by a sexy snake man whose name you can't even say. So then you move to a place like this, and it's all very clean and respectable and no one ever lets on how horny they are to try something new. And it's only ever women."

"They have *two*?!"

Geillis looked incredibly smug as she lounged in her chair. "Mhm. The lizard men too. Big ones, small ones, some with squishy little spikes. It's always a treat if you're not expecting it."

"So you're saying every human in town's only here because they want to be dicked down by other species?"

Geillis smiled, showing a hint of glinting fang. "I'm just saying . . . look, you know the one who comes in here every day, the fireman?" Violet bit her lip, flushing as she nodded. The dark-haired man who'd been in front of her in line the very first time she'd come into the Black Sheep did indeed come in nearly every day, at least every day the girls met up, always with that same wide smile and quicksilver sheen in his eye. He was a werewolf, she'd learned, from a prominent, wealthy family. "He's got a whole lot of brothers and they're *all* that scrummy. The one, he throws these parties, and I've heard it's like ancient Greece. Just naked women getting taken on hands and knees in the grass everywhere, and the closer they get to the full moon, the wilder it is. Humans come from towns away, all over! All hoping for an invite, because deep down, it's every girl's fantasy to be fucked by the big, bad wolf."

"I can't help but feel like there's a point you're trying to make."

"Has that big bull of yours rutted you yet?"

The elves at the next table turned disdainfully at the strangled noise that had come from her mouth, head dropping to hide in the crook of her arm as Geillis laughed. "I'm going to start keeping an ear to the ground in my complex, let you know if something opens up. Housing market 'round here is fierce. Because luvvie, once he does, you'll not be going back to humans, 's'all I'm saying."

She pulled on the bull's big testicles, spotted like his hide, as the Good Little Cow moaned. The sucking nozzle of the milking machine finished him off, and the light turned green. It had taken her the better part of three months, but she finally understood what Kirime had meant by saying their job wasn't sex work, not from the point of view of the technician. It might have been in the human communities, but things were different here, and Geillis was right. Different was good.

* * *

"I'm going to have the new girl shadow you for the rest of the afternoon, okay?"

The shift leader called out as soon as Violet entered the employee area, turning into the locker room before she answered. The patterned scrubs were discarded and dropped into the laundry cart, and Violet pulled a fresh set from the rack, solid lavender, before she was able to school her features into a mask of Kirime-like cheerfulness, turning to the shift leader. "Sounds good to me! Will she be with me the rest of the day?" She made an effort to keep her voice even and her tone nonchalant as she gathered up her charts, keeping her eyes averted, her lips pursing when her question was answered in the affirmative.

She didn't want the shift leader to question why she wouldn't want the brand new employee to be with her all day; didn't want her taking a closer look at the charts.

It was a Tuesday, the most unassuming day of the week. Past the Monday blahs and not far enough past the excruciating Wednesday ughs, with several days to endure before Rourke's standing appointment on Friday afternoons . . . but then Donnaxa had handed off her charts that morning, the purple sticker at the bottom of the stack instantly raising her heart rate and igniting her daydreams. She didn't know why he'd be visiting the farm so soon after his last appointment, if it was him at all, and the notion of having someone else there to disrupt their time together—disturbing their conversation, intruding on the false intimacy she'd created in her head—was most unwelcome.

She didn't think it was unreasonable to be upset, learning she was to have a shadow the entire day who would watch as she milked bull after bull, seeing the marked difference in the way she would handle the last client's cock, the way she would savor the time spent stroking him. *Or worse–she'll be the one doing the milking.* Violet remembered her first days of training, the way Rourke himself had been the first client she'd worked on. It was absurd to feel jealous, but her fists balled all the same.

"You'll get a training bonus to make up for the tip loss," the shift leader went on, confirming her fears. If you could trade off on every few clients that would be great—let her observe you, then let her take the next couple.

Don't shy away from feedback," she added, brow furrowing. "This one has technically already had two weeks of training, so she *should* know what to do, but I'm not ready to let her out on her own, if you know what I mean."

She hadn't, not at that point, but the reasons behind the shift leader's hesitation were made obvious as Violet observed the girl on the second client of the afternoon. She seemed to have no problem setting up the room, although she audited herself against the checklist infrequently. *Not an ideal situation, something that can be corrected with a reminder.* Her milking technique, however, left much to be desired. Up and down, up and down, a tight grip with no variation, she handled the cock belonging to one of the Earners with the same energy and excitement that one might undertake forced exercise, and Violet was uncomfortably reminded of her old university roommate's shake weights, and the way she'd mindlessly jiggle one in her hand as she watched soap operas between classes.

"So, did they tell you during your training that you should be checking the file for every client? You know they have preferences listed sometimes, right?"

The girl shrugged again, loading the used collection tank and tube onto the conveyor belt where it was whisked away for cleaning. "Yeah, I saw it. I was doing it, I thought."

Violet frowned. The mindless up-and-down motion the new girl's hands had adopted didn't come close to being what the client had requested, didn't even look pleasurable. *Maybe she's just bad at hand jobs . . . wrong place of employment, in that case. Maybe she'll be better on the next one.* One client turned into three, and Violet quickly discovered her optimism was misplaced.

"So, you're doing a really good job setting up the room," she began several minotaurs later as the girl executed the clean up protocols. The last two sessions had been heavily reliant on the use of the sucking nozzles of the machine to bring the bulls over the edge, and she knew the girl would not last long with her current method. "You've got a good handle on the machines and the process, so nice job . . . did you by chance watch the training videos?"

The girl was another human, something that would have thrilled her three months earlier, a fact that seemed oddly unimportant now. She'd been spending more and more time exploring Cambric Creek, preferring to undertake as many of her chores there as she could. She'd been giddy the first time she went up and down the aisles at the Food Gryphon, finding her own run-of-the-mill grocery items nestled in amongst exotic fruit nectars for moth and bat people, Molt-Ease bath products for those of the reptilian persuasion, toasted kelp crisps, unidentifiable breakfast foods, and bags of "double crunch cicadas in poppin' jalapeno."

There had been another human one evening, slowly making her way through the produce section with a tall mothman, absently *mhming* along to what sounded like a lecture on bees. Her eyes had met Violet's as they passed on opposite sides of a tower of bananas, and her smile had been kind and conspiratorial, an assumption that Violet was like her—a human who'd successfully broken through the barrier of this mixed-species society, so different from the world they were from. *Geillis really does have us all figured out.*

"Babe, are you gonna actually voice an opinion on what you want, or just talk about potter wasps all night?"

She had moved too far up the aisle to be able to hear the mothman's exasperated response, but smiled to herself, imagining passing the couple on another occasion, Rourke pushing the cart as she picked out pricey organic fruit, nodding to the other human over the bananas and sharing her conspiratorial smile, an acknowledgment of a club in which they were both members.

Being a human felt like less of a handicap now than it had several months ago, and while she was willing to cut this new human employee a generous amount of slack, it wasn't an excuse to not do the job well. She watched as the new girl wrinkled her nose in response to the question.

"Yeah, sort of. That lady's voice was so annoying though. I don't understand why it was so long."

Violet smiled woodenly, watching as the trainee gathered up the final chart of the day, bearing its purple sticker. "Well, I'll be honest, you need to watch them again. Your technique is lazy, and you're not paying attention to their charts. The notes are there for our benefit, you know. Get them in, get them out, and on with their day, so we can fit in more clients. You can't rely so much on the unit to do the work, and besides, a lot of the clients don't like for us to use them much." It was good advice, she told herself; maybe a little harsh, but necessary if the girl wanted to last. Unfortunately, her words were not received as well as she'd hoped.

The girl scoffed, wrinkling her nose. "Why does it matter? I thought as long as they come its fine."

"If that were true, why would they need us? If we're just going to slip the nozzle on two minutes after getting the clients in the chair, they could do away with our position entirely. We had to pass off two charts today—and that's fine, you're still in training, I guess. But it's not going to be fine in two weeks. You need to check yourself against the lists, and I strongly advise watching the training videos again . . . and I'm going to take the last chart. We're already running behind."

The only sound in the echoing hallway as they moved to the last collection room was the swish of her scrubs, the new girl trailing sullenly behind. Violet entered the room first, giving him a smile that she was grateful the other woman did not see.

"We have a trainee joining us today," she announced cheerfully, hoping her chipper, fake tone conveyed how she felt about the company. His head cocked curiously, his chocolate brown eyes tracking the young woman who slumped petulantly against the wall. "Why don't you get us set up," she instructed as Rourke stepped out of his pants. Violet listened to the sound of his heavy tread crossing to the breeding bench, the creak of the frame competing with the sound of the chrome tank being pulled from the rack and hooked into place.

"Well, I'm doing it. I have an appointment for this weekend. I'm taking the plunge."

"You're finally going to cut that scruffy hair?" she guessed, laughing when he made a noise of outrage, his broad nose wrinkling around the gold ring. His horns sliced through the air as he shook his head in annoyance and she

101

laughed.

"What? No! I'm getting the ring removed."

She wasn't sure how the contents of her chest managed to melt so completely, leaving behind that gooey marshmallow heat. "Congratulations," she murmured, feeling the trainee's eyes on her back. "That's a big step."

"It is," he agreed. "But it's overdue. And now there's an incentive to be free and clear. Symbolically back on the meat market." His rich voice enunciated each word clearly as if he were giving a PowerPoint presentation, selling the benefits of his ring removal, the reverberation of which she felt down to her core as he straddled the stocks, leaning over to peer down at her. She wondered if he could see the way her skin had flushed, if he was able to divine the reason.

"I thought maybe someone new was requesting me when I saw the sticker this morning," she added after a moment, as the other girl went through the motions of the setup checklist. Violet held her breath listening for his reaction. *Piquing his jealousy is a good way to remind your Capricorn lover to treasure his mate.* "A Tuesday notch on my dance card." A bullish snort was her only answer, his hooves scraping peevishly against the turf. "I'm glad it's not," she quickly added, keeping the second half of the website's advice in mind. "Although I don't know how I got lucky enough to see you twice in just a few days. "

A mollified grunt and then he was leaning forward, settling his weight against the bench and filling the hole. She had thought about his cock all afternoon, watching the inefficient way the new girl manhandled client after client. He was thick with arousal, the veins snaking around his girth seeming especially prominent. Every minotaur who visited the farm had the same anatomy—vaguely human-like in shape, with thick mid-shaft swells and bulbous heads, but his . . . she would be able to pick his particular endowment out of a lineup with ease.

"You mentioned wanting to go exploring on weekends, I assumed that meant you're off then. I took a gamble that you'd be here."

"Does this mean you won't be coming later in the week?"

His voice dropped, deeper in pitch and lower in volume, stern and pointed, meant only for her ears. "Oh, I'll be here. I've been needing to masturbate more often lately. This weekend the urge was especially . . . *demanding.* I thought coming in for a good draining might help take the edge off until Friday."

Her hands were trembling when she raised her oiled gloves to cup his sac, full and heavy and hot with need. *Coffee and an argument with you on Friday and then frantically beating off all weekend. Poor baby . . .* The thought of him taking his huge cock in hand, pumping it as he thought of her, wasting his valuable release because he was overcome with horniness—it was a terrible fucking day to have a shadow following her every move. She wondered how he pleasured himself, if he used a firm, overhand stroke or a softer touch, mimicking the inefficient grip of her small hands, drawing out the process and edging himself until he came with a messy eruption. Dragging her nails lightly down his plump testicles, she bounced them against her palms, grinning when he growled.

"They definitely feel very full. We'll have to make sure we give you a good, deep milking today, help tide you over until Friday."

"And then the ring comes out Saturday."

This was their foreplay, she thought, her stomach swooping over the implication of his words. "And then you're back on the meat market Saturday." *Free and clear.* She took a deep breath, glad for the mask that hid her smile, hoping the new girl wouldn't notice the affection with which she gripped his cock, and slowly began to stroke.

Chapter 11

"*You.*"

His voice was accusing, and an affronted scowl creased over his broad, handsome face. Violet noticed immediately the absence of the ring in his nose, the unencumbered nostrils flared in indignation, feeling a pang of regret that she'd not been there to see him in the days following its removal.

You don't need a one-sided infatuation, remember? The voice in her head was right, she reminded herself. The time away had been good for clearing her head of the cobwebs of senseless lust she'd allowed to spool and stretch, obliterating her good sense and professionalism. Being back under her parents' roof and sleeping in her childhood bed for the preceding two weeks had done wonders for shaking thoughts of the messy-haired minotaur away, reminding herself of the bills she needed to pay, the career she needed to actually start someday, the plan she had for her life. *Pining after a client isn't part of the plan, especially one like this.* She exhaled sharply, knowing the voice was right. *He's probably been out with a dozen different women since you've been gone. Putting himself back on the meat market, right?* Glancing over her shoulder, she made a show of looking around, as if he might be referring to someone behind her.

"Where have you been? I had to practically twist someone's arm off just to find out if you still worked here."

Violet bit her lip, trying to imagine him cajoling information from the new girl, remaining as stiff and silent as all the other Clockwatchers during the two appointments that she'd missed. "They probably didn't tell you much, it's against company policy to divulge any information about employees. Especially to a client," she added, reinforcing his status for his benefit as much as her own.

His scowl deepened and she very nearly laughed aloud at the deep crease between his narrowed eyes, his wide mouth pulling into an exaggerated frown. *He's adorable when he pouts.* The thought came to her unbidden, pulling an invisible cord of tension behind her navel, unraveling her resolve like a kitten with a ball of yarn. It didn't matter how many pep talks she'd given herself over the past week, didn't matter what she told herself about the futility of her crush or the inappropriateness of harboring such feelings for a client—the instant the traitorous thought crossed her mind, all of her willpower went crashing to the ground. He'd been there with her for every minute she'd been away, imagining his arms coming around her when she cried and the warmth of his hide pressed against her at night, and it was foolish to attempt to persuade herself otherwise.

"Don't give me that. I can't believe you literally left me in the clutches of that amateur. I was *chafed* after the last time. Chafed!"

She was unable to hold in her laughter as she hooked the collection tank into the unit, ensuring the bottle rack was full and the hoses secure before turning to let him see her eye roll at his dramatics. It was the first time she'd laughed in what felt like ages, and the fact that he'd been the one to invoke it felt significant.

Despite it seeming like the week had already been endless, it was only her second day back to work after being absent for two weeks, and although she'd never be able to prove it, Violet was certain that Magda had given her the most challenging rotations since she returned. The very first client the previous day had been one of the most vocal of the good little cows, lowing enthusiastically as she stroked him, and things had quickly deteriorated from there.

"Ohhh, milk me, please milk me . . . you're going to milk me dry," the minotaur had moaned, bucking wildly against the padded stocks above her. She had begun to compare every minotaur she worked on to Rourke, comparing their endowments and the way they felt in her hands. That bull's cock had been long and pink and thin, like a writhing tentacle. Her hands had missed the heavy weight she'd grown to prefer as she struggled to maintain a rhythm wringing the slippery, snake-like appendage, in between the constant encouragement they liked to receive. Catching hold of him once he'd begun to buck and thrust left her feeling like a rodeo clown, and Violet was certain she'd been less than gentle in jamming the sucking nozzle down his length, but she was past caring by then. It had set the tone for the rest of her shift as she handled one challenging client after the next, and today had not been much better.

It had been a long few weeks.

Her great-aunt's death had been unexpected. When her maternal grand-mother had died when she was a child, her sister had filled the hole left behind for Violet and her mother both. Aunt Gracie had always been more like a grandmother to her—baking cookies on Sundays, there for all of her accomplishments, both great and small. The call from her mother had given her time to fly home to say goodbye, for which she was grateful, staying to help her parents with the unplanned-for arrangements. People who didn't know her well didn't seem to expect that the loss of great aunt or uncle would affect her much, and it was exasperating and uncomfortable to explain; she didn't know any of her co-workers well enough to let them see her cry, and she knew that she *would* cry if she needed to explain beyond "there was a death in the family." Adding on the frustration of two long, challenging days' worth of clients had her on the edge, and all she wanted to do was collapse against the big minotaur before her, bury her face against his broad chest, and never let go.

That, she reminded herself with a swallow, was impossible, and she had a job to do.

"Poor thing," she laughed, ignoring his question and flashing a grin back at his scowl before ducking beneath the bench. The sight of his cock was like greeting an old friend, and she had to fight the urge to lean forward and press a kiss to the tip. "We'll have to be extra gentle on your delicate, chafed bits."

The lubricant the farm supplied was far thicker than anything she'd ever illicitly purchased at the small pharmacy near her apartment, thick and viscous with a pleasing slip and slide. Pumping a bit more into her gloved palm than she usually used, she slickened her hands before wrapping them around his thick shaft, her sigh of contentment echoed from overhead. It was the end of the day, Violet reminded herself, and there was no other client booked for this room. A plentiful speedy collection was what she strove to achieve each day . . . but it had been a long two weeks, and she was tired. Tired and frustrated and there was no one working that would think to come to the collection room to see what was taking so long.

She'd earned this, and she wasn't inclined to rush.

"The first client I had today was new. Like, new new. He'd never done this before."

She tightened her grip slightly as she slid her slickened palms against him, running her thumb up the thick vein that snaked up his shaft until she reached the tip. Reversing direction, she worked his foreskin back, letting her palm press into his shiny, exposed head until he hissed.

"I take it things didn't go well?"

She smiled at the roughness in his voice. She intended on enjoying his milking session and wanted him to as well. "Oh, it did not. Not at all." Talking as she stroked him seemed to be a new, previously undiscovered level of intimacy, and she could easily imagine herself having the conversation in bed on a Sunday morning, curled against his side as her hands moved, feeling the hot huff of his breath against her. It was a cozy thought, a warm thought, and she closed her eyes, immersing herself in the daydream fully.

She could almost feel the silky-coarse hair that covered him, imagined rubbing her nose against his chest, right above his heartbeat as she moved her hands, could feel the weight of the blankets and the strength in his arms, casually curled around her. She held his cock with both hands now, her thumbs moving in rhythmic circles at the base of his head, pressing into his frenulum. Lazy love-making would follow, feeling the cool sheets at her back as he rolled her gently, his heavy weight settling over her in a giant bed, something designed for larger species, one that wouldn't even fit into her little apartment.

"He literally had no clue. I had to instruct him to take his pants off, show him how to get into the chair." The young bull had possessed the odd combination of cocky swagger and wide-eyed confusion, and she'd blown out an impatient breath, aggravated that she was being set up to have a repeat of the previous day's annoyance. If he'd been a bit more humble, she might have gone easier on him, might have given him the practiced, cheerful smile she'd learned from Kirime and the fox-faced woman in the training videos, but he'd had a leering grin when she'd entered the room, his hands on his hips as he surveyed the collection floor.

"He lost his erection...twice!"

Rourke huffed, and she was able to see the edge of his horns as he shook his head. The minotaur from that afternoon had lost his cockiness the second his pants had come off, and he'd stood there expectantly as if she were going to climb the staircase to the upper lever and jerk him off right there. "And then . . . *then!* He finished with absolutely zero warning. Got some on my scrubs before I was able to get the nozzle on him. Half of what he was supposed to be paid for wound up in the laundry cart."

"You're not trying to one-up me, are you?" he demanded. "Because I got stuck with Stiff Grip Sally for two weeks and I thought she circumcised me at one point."

Violet let go of him, hunching as she laughed, shoulders shaking, envisioning the new girl's shake weight motion. "Oh noooo!" she cried, eyes streaming with her mirth. "Well, we can't have that . . . tell me if this is too much pressure, okay?"

She slid the tightened ring of her fingers down his fat shaft, relishing the familiar weight and heft in her hands before stretching her fingers and tickling at the underside of his sac. He would press into her slowly, letting her adjust to his insane girth; would seat himself fully with a grunt that would sound very much like the one he'd just given as she cupped his balls, pulling them slowly, giving him a bit of the stretch she knew he liked. He would fill her entirely, stretching her far beyond what she thought capable, but she would be used to the feel of him by then, the heavy weight of him, and when he would begin to move within her, her head would drop back in ecstasy, her hands tightening around his wide shoulders or gripping his broad horns.

"You're perfect."

The domed head of his cock seemed extra appealing that day, the tips of her fingers grazing it gently, teasing his foreskin back and forth, up and down, caressing the inside of the sensitive sheath until he groaned. *Circumcising this would have been a crime*, she thought, sliding the loose skin back until his full head popped free, like an especially delicious mushroom sprouting from the earth, beckoning her tongue to lick away the pearlescent moisture at its winking slit. She would enjoy tonguing him slowly, licking against his frenulum in a constant movement, the same movement her thumb took then, back and forth, over and over, sucking him into her mouth when he grunted in pleasure.

She would enjoy tasting him, but that would be later; a different time, she thought, returning to her daydream in progress. She began to twist up his shaft, running her hands one after another in a continuous flow, constant stimulation. Above her, Rourke groaned. His wide hips began to cant lightly against the padded breeding stocks, the same way his hips would thrust against her body, slow and deliberate and deep, always so in control, his rough, bovine tongue tasting the salt of her skin as he kissed her neck. Violet was able to hear her own cries of pleasure, the mindless begging that would fall from her lips; the baritone of his own deep groans and animalistic grunts as he fucked her, pounding into her with the same deliberate, measured force with which he rutted against the breeding bench. His heavy balls would hit her skin with every thrust, the percussive slap of them an obscene music that would fill the room, fat and full to bursting as he fucked her into the mattress, chasing his release and making her see stars.

She'd missed him, missed him *so* much, and seeing him—talking with him, flirting with him, hearing the sharp bark of his voice and feeling its reverberation down her back—felt like coming home. The realization hit her like a punch to the gut; the knowledge that while she'd been home with her family—mourning their loss, going through old photo albums and helping her mother clean out drawers, wishing she'd called more often and had come home sooner—she'd been thinking of him . . . but not like *this*. She had envisioned going back to her room with the little undersized bed every night and collapsing into his arms, losing herself in his calm control, feeling the heat of his mouth as he kissed away her tears. She hadn't missed *this*, but she had missed his stern voice and deep huffs of laughter, missed their banter and his messy hair and shining chocolate eyes. In her fantasy she would make breakfast together, feeding each other bites of chocolate croissants or blueberry-stuffed muffins, sipping gourmet coffee from the Black Sheep Beanery. They'd go back to bed to snuggle and talk and watch nostalgic movies as the sky outside darkened, but first . . . first he would fuck her until they were both satisfied, filling her with spurt after spurt of his extremely valuable seed.

His deep groan brought her back to the present, his solid, heavy thrusts against the padded breeding bench an echo of her daydream, and she worked the buzzing nozzle over the head of his cock with no time to spare. He continued to rock against her hands when the green light clicked on, lowing as he throbbed in her hands, and *gods* how she'd missed him. She wanted to know everything about him—how he liked his eggs and what he would feel like pressed to her side at night; the roughness of his tongue, how he took care of his horns, if he was close to his family and if he would turn her over his knee, as Geillis had suggested. Following the pulse of his balls as his thrusts began to weaken, she found and pressed her thumb against the visibly throbbing point behind his sac, massaging into his prostate, her pussy clenching when he bucked in response. His hooves scraped for purchase against the footrest and he groaned again, filling the machine with a fresh torrent of semen as she pressed against his sweet spot, squeezing her thighs together in time to the ropes of white splattering the glass. A click and whir from the collection unit made her jump, and she turned sharply, just in time to see the second bottle rotating into place.

She'd never had reason to use both of the label stickers that came affixed to the files, but there was a first time for everything, she thought ruefully.

He said nothing as she cleaned him off, giving the customary squeeze with which she always ended things, and remained quiet as she tagged the two bottles, the second barely filled to the quarter line. Turning back to the breeding bench, she was able to see his wide horns still there, laying stock still.

"I feel like I should have paid for that," he groaned, remaining slumped against the bench as she walked up the small staircase, coming up to his level for the very first time. She realized, freezing on the steps, that from this vantage point, she had a perfect view of his rounded backside and thick thighs, completing the fantasy of what it might be like to have him in her bed.

"I think you may have killed me."

"You sure are bossy for a corpse."

His messy hair tumbled into his eyes as he raised himself at last, keeping her locked in his gaze as he pushed himself from the bench, grunting as his back cracked when he twisted. His cock swayed between his thighs, soft and spent and still completely enormous, a hypnotic pendulum as he staggered the half-dozen paces across the room to where his pants rested over the hair back. She watched in fascination as he carefully guided his hooves through each leg, palming his tail and smoothing it through the small slit in the fabric's seat, bending to fasten and secure each pantleg over his jutting hocks. Dress shirt tucked in and smoothed, cock tucked away and fly zipped, he didn't look up until he was bucking his belt, and Violet could almost convince herself that they were in some cozy little domestic tableau together, dressing for work before he kissed her goodbye.

"It's strange," he rumbled, adjusting his watchband, the picture of brusque professionalism. "You see someone every week, you talk to them, they're a part of your routine, your schedule. They become part of your life. You share a certain level of intimacy with them. You miss them when they're gone. You can almost convince yourself you know them, because you start to fill in blanks on your own, but you never *really* know."

A vice had fastened over her heart at his words, so similar to what she herself had been thinking over, and her face felt over-warm; the soft, hazy glow of her daydream giving the past hour and her cheeks both a rosy flush, her eyes pricking with tears.

"You never answered me. Where were you?"

In an instant, the rosy flush fled, leaving the tears behind. She remembered that he'd not actually been there to comfort her over the last two weeks and that he was right—he only knew her in the context of this place, of this job, and that wasn't likely to change.

"I-there was a death in the family."

His broad face sobered in a flash, his forehead wrinkling. "I'm so sorry to hear that. My condolences. Was it someone close?"

She had already turned, wondering what had possessed her to come up to the top level, robbing herself of the protective barrier of the breeding bench, where she could hide away with her fantasies and not face up to the reality that it was all they were. Tears blurred her vision and her voice seemed to stick in her throat as she nodded, and she jolted when his giant hand rested on her shoulder, heavy and warm, the way she knew it always would be. His eyes, when she turned, were filled with compassion.

"Let's get out of here, come grab a coffee with me. You can tell me about them."

He was close enough for her to feel the heat of his body. The pad of his thumb was velvety soft as he cradled the side of her face in his huge hand, catching one of her tears and smoothing it away against her skin. She'd not expected such softness from him, always so sharp and brusque, but her head tipped up all the same, willing to meet his mouth if he'd leaned down just a fraction more. She was still able to smell the coffee from her dream, the little local coffee roaster's beans, made in his kitchen as she leaned against him, her face pressed to his strong back. His thunderclap voice too had softened, deep and comforting, with no hint of demand, and she nodded, wanting nothing more than to be there with him, be somewhere—anywhere—other than the farm.

"Go on then, punch out. I'll get us a table. Probably going to need to flip over a booth of teenagers, but it's fine, they'll bounce."

She could feel the weight of his hand on her back as she drifted down the steps as if the heat of him had burned an imprint on her skin, a glow she was certain the whole world could see as she collected her things and clocked out with her heart in her mouth. *This is it, you can do this. Coffee first. Then tomorrow, you can lock yourself into his house and never, ever leave.* It was, Violet was certain, a perfect plan.

Chapter 12

The soft pressure of his thumb was driving her crazy. Around them, the Black Sheep Beanery buzzed with its normal hustle and bustle of patrons gossiping in clusters and jockeying for space. She recognized the lab coat-wearing orc at the table across from theirs from her previous visits, laughing with a human woman in scrubs not unlike those she wore at the farm, and somewhere behind them a harpy cackled. Rourke had taken her hand in his when her voice had hitched, telling him of the final days spent with her aunt in the hospital; enfolding it in his giant palm in the center of the small table as tears spilled over her lashes, recounting the funeral and the days that had followed. He'd not released her as the conversation shifted, and the gentle, velvet pressure of his thumb circling on the inside of her wrist was driving her to dizzy distraction.

"I have a sweet tooth," he'd announced when she first slid into the chair across from him, tucked into a corner of the always-busy shop. "I wasn't sure what you might like, so help yourself to both." A chocolate croissant dusted with powdered sugar sat on one of two plates in the center of the table, and on the other Violet recognized one of the caramel pecan twists he'd ordered several weeks earlier. "The coffee order just came up a minute ago, so it should still be hot."

Her cup was plugged with a steam keeper, a stack of napkins sat between the plates with both a knife and fork. *A details-oriented perfectionist.* It was enough to make her swoon. "Word on the street is you're going to turn into one of these twists." Their situation was ridiculous, Violet considered as he clucked his tongue. She knew how the heft of his heavy sac felt in her hands, knew how much pull he enjoyed on his hot testicles before his muscles would tighten; knew the spot on his cockhead where he was most sensitive, knew how tight her hands needed to be to make him low deeply. She knew what his orgasm felt like, the pulse of his blood as he came, the way he turned boneless for a moment after . . . it was ludicrous to know so many intimate details about the most private parts of him, and to still have known so little about him. *Time to change all that.*

"You said your grandmother was human?"

"Mhm, she was from town and my grandfather grew up on the settlement. It's pertinent to keep in mind that this is in the backwoods of the backwater middle of nowhere. They had over three hundred acres of farmland, my parents built their house on one end of it and my cousins lived on the other end. I would read books about kids that would just go out and play without having to muck out stalls and collect in the chicken coops and I assumed it was make-believe."

The image of him as a child with tiny nubs for horns and soft, lamb-like ears made her stomach somersault as she laughed. "I didn't realize minotaurs lived in groups like that, like orcs?" She tried to envision the patrons of the farm all going back to the same little neighborhood, and thought that much testosterone in one place was a recipe for disaster.

"They normally don't. This was a very isolated community, human towns all over. Goddess knows why other species stayed put in areas like that, but if they did, they usually stuck together." His voice held its usual matter-of-factness, but he hesitated for a moment before continuing. "It's not always safe to be surrounded by humans that way, that's why you see things like cervitaur herds and wolf packs."

He'd been married for nearly five years, had started his own company, owned a home in Cambric Creek. He was a proper adult, a thought that left her shifting against the seat of her chair. She drove a car that had belonged to her aunt, the same generic orange juice was still in her refrigerator, and had to save her tip money to even be able to come to this pricey little gourmet roaster. *He is so out of your league, this night is going to end with him shaking*

115

your hand so he can enjoy the weekly hand job with a clear conscience . . . but he'd still not released her hand, still stroked the inside of her wrist like she were a kitten in his palm, and the unexpected tenderness from him—always so stern, so in control—had french braided her lungs together, leaving her heart to thump pitifully from within the tangle.

"I'm an only child, so was my mom, so I didn't grow up with a lot of family around. My mom wants me to move back home, to be closer and I know it's because she's lonely, she doesn't *really* want me to give up doing something I love . . . but I don't have a career, this is just a job, so I feel guilty. I'm a millennial, being anxious and guilty is my birthright, I guess, right? But I *do* love it here." Her mother, unsurprisingly, had conspired with Mrs. Tinsely, and she'd found herself sitting across from Carson Tinsely in a small cafe a week after the funeral. The conversation with her junior high crush had been stilted and strange, completely unlike the time spent with the big minotaur. "I love learning about the different cultures and the food . . . it's amazing that so many different species can come together here, it makes me want to explore *every*thing!"

"It's not always roses and sunshine," he'd cautioned with another one of those deep chuckles, a vibrating rumble she wanted to feel against her skin. "Some people don't wear pants. Now, I'm willing to admit that I've lived around humans my whole life, and I understand the way majority culture tends to bleed into everything, but covering your ass in public should be the basic entry point for society, in my opinion. So . . . there's that. But it's a nice place. It can be trying, having neighbors celebrating random holidays that involve screaming at the moon on a Tuesday, but for the most part everyone tries to get along."

The sky outside was a wash of pink and gold, the sun a brilliant orange orb, slowly sinking to crimson. More than an hour had passed, she realized, yet there had been no awkward pauses or silences; no strained laughter or stilted conversation.

"Look, I don't know how inappropriate this is or not, but I'm a bit past the point of caring."

She jumped at the sudden bark of his deep voice and he paused, releasing her hand to drag a big hand over his face. "I meant to ask you after I got the ring out, that was the whole point in doing it. I-I don't like not having the answers I require, and you are just . . . a very intriguing question mark. I missed you, you know. When you were gone."

Her heart folded in on itself, the notion that he had been thinking of her the same way she thought of him, trying to fill in the blanks in his head. "I missed you too."

"Well . . . I'm free and clear now, and I'd like to get to know you better." A bit of that authoritative thunderclap had returned and she straightened in her seat, pressing her thighs together at the hint of demand as he continued. "I don't want to make things awkward, and I don't want to jeopardize anything for you at work. If you want me to pause my appointments for the time being, I will." She shook her head, the ability to speak suddenly deserting her, and the corners of his wide mouth lifted slightly. "I'd like to get to know you, outside of the farm, and I hope my feelings aren't one-sided." A flash of white teeth as she continued to flounder mutely, her head bobbing in a nod before shaking again, unsure which sentiment with which she was agreeing. "But I don't think they are. Would you like to have dinner with me this weekend, Violet?"

The sound of her name in his deep voice turned her into a puddle. She had no doubt that if she said no, he'd never mention it again, that she'd likely never see him again at all. She might have gone on pining forever, building castles of dreams in the sky that she would never act on . . . but she had always been a sucker for authority. She'd been certain that he could ask anything of her in that commanding voice and she'd be helpless to say yes, just as she was certain his sheets would be cool against her back and his weight a comforting heaviness at her side. *Rourke.*

"I'd love that."

V

Part Five

Chapter 13

"Remember, just get up before dessert and take your knickers off in the loo. When you come back to the table, give your old bully boy a present. He'll barely be able to wait until the check comes, guaranteed."

Violet blew a hard breath out her nose, squinting in the bright, overhead light. "Don't you think you should focus on what you're doing? I won't have to worry about taking my underwear off if I'm in the emergency room because you waxed off half my labia."

The vampire rolled her eyes, taking up the tongue depressor of wax once more. Violet wasn't sure how she'd let Geillis talk her into this, and half-suspected that she'd fallen prey to a vampire glamour. *No, you didn't. You're letting her do it because you're a horny idiot.* The voice in her head, she had to admit, was right, at least this time. Geillis had asked if she'd made sure to be freshly waxed for the big night, and she'd responded with a typical deer-in-the-headlights look of panic, for even though she was certain it wouldn't actually matter, she'd never been waxed in her life and now that the idea had been put out into the universe, she desperately wanted to be. That sort of pricey salon service was definitely *not* in her budget, even as a splurge, and so Geillis had volunteered, insisting that she'd had salon experience over her vast, long, vampiric life.

It wasn't until she was laying on the kitchen table, naked from the waist down with her knee pressed to her ear, that she remembered Geillis had been turned in the 1980's and was around the same age as Violet's mother.

"Just hold bloody still, I'm almost finished!"

She closed her eyes and held her breath as the waxing paper was pressed to her skin, trying to focus on the exact scenario Geillis described, the one that had caused her to be in such a position. She wanted to be stretched by his big bullcock, wanted him to fuck her into next season with those measured, pounding thrusts, but lately, the notion of him bathing her sex with his hot tongue was all she could think of, and her judgment had abandoned her. *Tonight. Something's going to happen tonight.* She had lost count of the dinner dates and mid-day lunches, the romantic excursions through the quaint little town, and the gallery visits in the city. He'd wanted to get to know her, for her to get to know him, for them to know each other outside of the milking facility and the heightened sexuality that had permeated their interactions for the previous several months, and she appreciated his circumspection more than she could articulate . . . but if the night didn't end with her screaming his name as she came around his cock, Violet was certain she was going to perish from terminally unmet sexpectations.

* * *

Their first date had been at a cozy little trattoria around the corner from her apartment in the city, and he'd been a perfect gentleman.

Bridgeton boasted a multi-species population, like most large cities, and although humans were the majority, she had begun to pay closer attention after his comments about majority culture as she went about her days, noticing the goblins and trolls who were nearly invisible in the backdrop of the city's hustle and bustle. She'd discovered that her little corner bodega carried a small selection of items similar to those she'd seen at the Food Gryphon—kelp-flavored crisps and oddly-colored drinks, all stuffed on the lowest shelf at the back of the store. Violet had watched open-mouthed one evening as a petite goblin with wide hips and a sleeve of colorful tattoos, clutching the hand of a small child entered the store while she was leaning into the ice cream case, moving with purpose to the back aisle. She had stepped back with her strawberry crunch cone, watching surreptitiously as the goblin woman bent, releasing hold of her child and practically needing to kneel to load her shopping basket with items from the bottom shelf.

She'd let the woman go ahead of her in line as the little boy grew fidgety, and the whole episode had left her discomfited. She tried to imagine being forced to do all of her grocery shopping at the over-priced mini-mart without having half a dozen other options, and remembered the conversation she'd overheard in the locker room one day as Kirime and one of the other technicians bemoaned the skyrocketing property market in Cambric Creek. *No wonder other species want to move there.*

He'd met her at the restaurant that Saturday night, standing sentinel on the sidewalk as she scurried across the street, blushing that he'd beaten her when she lived right around the corner. *Of course mister always-in-control is punctual, why are you surprised?!* She asked about where he'd lived in the city, realizing from his description of the neighborhood that it wasn't terribly far from her own apartment, explaining why he'd been immediately familiar with her suggestion.

"My ex-wife kept the townhouse," he went on, eyes dropping to the wine glass before him, "and my business is in Cambric Creek, so I tend to not have much reason to come into the city these days . . . until now," he conceded, flashing her one of those brilliant smiles, transforming him into a softer version of himself for the space of a heartbeat.

"What happened?" she'd blurted, desperately needing an answer to the question that had been turning over in her mind since that first night she'd met him for coffee. She had come home from the coffee shop that night nearly floating over the way the evening had ended, immediately bee-lining to her laptop to stalk him online. She wasn't especially proud that she had developed a knack for digging up dirt on people, but over the years she had discovered a talent for rooting out extended family member's social media, long-outdated resumes, and forgotten accounts with only the barest hint of information on her target. She knew his birthday, and now she knew his name. It was more than enough.

In the end, she'd found his ex-wife first.

Most people's accounts were set to private these days, circumventing online snoops like her, but the glamorous woman with the crimson smile had public-facing everything. Profile after profile, different social platforms that all linked together, Violet paged through the highly-curated, glossy life of her bull's former spouse, feeling more and more like a drab little mouse with every click.

Her mind had supplied her with the image of someone tall and slender, like the tiefling at the coffee shop, clad in expensive business attire with a stern expression, identical to his, well-matched in profession. The voluptuous beauty posing beside a green-tiled swimming pool—her long, ebony hair wrapped in a turban with oversized, ivory sunglasses hiding her eyes and red-painted lips stretched wide—bore no resemblance to the phantom lover she'd dreamt up. Human-looking, save for the cow-like tail that swished behind her and the curious, dark shadow of her back, which wasn't turned towards the camera in any shot. *Well, he doesn't dislike human anatomy, at least you know that much.* As she toggled back and forth between social platforms, scrolling through the endless feed of selfies and staged photos, Violet noticed the complete absence of real life—no family outings, no milestones or pets, no hint of the man with whom this smiling woman had once shared her life. The oldest photo in the feed was dated three years prior, and in those first few dozen, the other woman's make-up was a bit more subdued, her eyelashes not yet lengthened with extensions, her lips stained a dark berry-red. *He said he's been divorced for two years.*

She had recognized the mark of someone reinventing herself and understood the compulsion well. It would have been easy to do, had she found that dream job she'd been expecting right out of school—filling her social feeds with artsy, black and white photos of Bridgeton and her life in the big city, the over-priced burnt coffee from up the street balancing on a ledge overlooking the high rises across the water. It would have been easy to hide her humble beginnings and human family . . . just as this woman had completely hidden away any hint of whom she might have been, when she'd been his wife. Her stomach tightened and flipped, unliking the idea of him being the life that had been worth hiding.

There were no photos of him to speak of, and no social media accounts she could find under his name, which didn't actually surprise her a bit. Too brusque, too professional for that. The closest revelation she stumbled on was a comment on one of the oldest pictures in the other woman's feed; a clueless, inappropriate comment from someone who appeared to be a relative, damning evidence that he had existed at all. *I'm so sorry to hear about you and Rourke.* She'd straightened in her seat at the discovery, quickly clicking on the profile of the commenter. A dozen or so photos of landscape and several children, all girls, all with the same, swishing tails behind them. The pictures had no filters and were of an odd, hasty composition, the mark of an older user who was unfamiliar with the photo platform's highly curated vibe.

Searching the woman's name, she quickly turned up a profile on CrowdJournal, more widely used with her own parent's demographic. *Paydirt*. Hundreds of photos, going back years. It didn't take her long to find what she was looking for. *Veleena's handfasting*. The album only consisted of half a dozen photos, and only one with him. He towered over the bride, looking as neat and severe as he did when he loomed over her every Friday, if not a bit younger. The bride herself was a revelation. Clear-eyed and smiling softly, with none of the dramatic makeup or brash confidence on display in her current photos, she'd gazed up at the big minotaur before her looking like a completely different person.

Violet had gone to bed that night wondering what had happened; if this other woman had decided to become someone new before their marriage had ended, if they'd *each* become someone new, and the people they'd become after their vows simply hadn't worked together. Violet found that she couldn't think badly of the woman in the photos, for she herself seemed completely different compared to the person she'd been only six months earlier; before she'd known about minotaur milking farms and vampire restaurants, when she'd been ignorant to the way her neighbors of different species lived and had been blind to her human privilege. She'd not be able to go back, that was certain, no matter how much her mother and Carson Tinsely from up the street might have wished it, so she could not fault this other woman for reinventing her life in a way that made her happy, and she clearly seemed happy in the multitude of photos.

His mouth had pressed and his head had cocked consideringly. "We had very different priorities by the end. It wasn't any one big thing, it's not like someone was cheating or anything like that, we just . . . it was one of those things. She wanted to travel, I was just starting my business. All of her friends were single, I was always working . . . we drifted apart and pretty soon we were strangers who happened to live together. I was far too boring for her, in any case."

"Well, I have great news for you, because I'm the most boring person I know."

The rich sound of his laughter had spilled over her like a thick flood of dark chocolate, warmer and more vibrant than the quiet huffs she'd heard at the farm, melting her insides in a way that was becoming deliciously familiar as he caught her pinky with his index finger on the edge of the table. "You don't bore me. Not in the slightest."

If she'd thought at the time that the two bottles of red wine they'd shared would have lubricated the path back to her bed, she might have been disappointed. He'd walked her to the door of her building, and the invitation to come up had never had a chance to escape her mouth, swallowed up by his lips as they'd been. His mouth was wider than those belonging to any of her previous partners, wide enough to engulf hers completely, but his lips were soft and his wide tongue hot and rough, and he'd kissed her until she was clinging to him and dizzy.

"I've wanted to do that for a very long time." Deep and dark, his voice had rumbled against her exactly the way she'd suspected it might, as she'd fisted the front of his shirt in an attempt to stay upright. "I enjoyed spending time with you, Violet. I hope we can do it again soon."

* * *

Soon had been four days later, when she'd met him for a pre-dinner drink at a crowded happy hour pub in Cambric Creek's bustling downtown, before walking hand-in-hand to one of the many farm-to-table restaurants the town boasted. She'd been keenly aware of their size difference when he'd lifted her like a doll, as she struggled to climb onto a bar stool designed for a much larger species. His thickly muscled arm had scooped her up in a blink, a huge hand in the center of her back until she balanced upon the seat sufficiently.

"What's that drink with the soda and syrup you make for kids? With the cherries?"

The server, a fleet-footed faun had cocked their eyebrow, making the piercings there bounce. "A lulabelle?"

"That's the one. See that table of elves at the edge of the bar there? I want

127

to send one to the blonde in the blue dress. No alcohol, and if you can add one of those little paper umbrellas, all the better."

The satyr had narrowed their eyes dubiously, looking from Violet to the big minotaur before turning to put the order in with a shrug.

"Did you just buy another woman a drink right in front of me?"

"I did, but just wait. She'll be stomping over here in a minute. This way we can make introductions without needing to get up." He'd leaned down then, easily covering the distance between them at the small table, and she'd barely had time to suck in a breath before he was kissing her, stealing the air from her lungs and doing nothing to ensure the continued dryness of her panties. "Thank you for meeting me tonight. I know Wednesdays aren't exactly the most romantic date night, but the idea of not seeing you until next week didn't sit well."

The baritone vibration of his voice went directly between her thighs, her head practically lolling as the edge of his muzzle grazed the shell of her ear.

"I can't believe you have to cancel for Friday." The news that she'd not be seeing him at the farm that week had been a crushing blow, and she'd been mourning the opportunity to milk him, the first time she'd have done so since he'd come to meet her in the city. Taking his cock in her hands and listening to his tightly controlled gasps and grunts—now that she knew exactly where her head came up on his chest, now that knew he preferred to start his meal with dessert, now that she knew how searingly hot his mouth was on hers—was the most erotic thing she could imagine, and she'd been looking forward to his weekly appointment since he'd left her on her doorstep the previous Saturday.

"You didn't think of taking this trip while Stiff Grip Sally was covering for me?" She hadn't had the chance to fully appreciate his full-throated laugh, as a woman had appeared at his elbow, petite and full-figured with long, tapered ears, her sapphire eyes narrowed as she jabbed Rourke's shoulder.

"You know, joke's on you because I actually like these." As if to prove her point, the elf tipped back the fruit-adorned drink she carried, smacking her lips defiantly. "Please tell me you didn't tell Xenna I'd absolutely be at her party."

"Because that sounds like something I'd do, after all. Do you mean to tell me Mr. Perfect isn't overjoyed for the opportunity to ooze and schmooze with the whole neighborhood?"

The elf cocked her head, considering, and Violet had used the opportunity to gawk. Her dark blue eyes were wide-set and fringed in pale lashes, with a spray of freckles over her tiny button nose. She was lovely, and Violet was forced to wonder if she looked as drab and boring in comparison as she felt. "Actually, he would, you're right." Her lips curled into a self-satisfied smile as Rourke snorted, and then the elf's eyes turned, taking Violet in for the first time.

"Hi, I'm Lurielle. Are you planning on making introductions, Rourke?"

She was introduced to the infamous neighbor, the full apples of other woman's cheeks rosy-pink as she smiled, blue eyes flashing as she looked from human to minotaur with an approving hum. "Violet, I'll warn you now—he's *very* bossy, and if you go to get ice cream, he *will* harass you for a taste of your cone. It doesn't matter if he sampled it at the shop, he's greedy. But he's a very good neighbor, so I'd appreciate it if you didn't convince him to move away. Oh! We just got a new patio set, you'll both have to come over for drinks and dinner. Khash likes to pretend that he single-handedly wrestled down a mastodon every time he turns on the grill, it'll be great."

She'd left the table soon after, extracting a promise from Rourke that they'd come over some evening soon, before disappearing through the press of bodies to return to her friends. Violet liked her enormously.

Dinner had been just up the block on the vibrant little town's Main Street, and when the bill arrived, she'd attempted to pull a handful of carefully folded bills from her wristlet, before he'd stopped her.

"No, that's absolutely not happening. Put that away."

She'd not thought about it until the day after their first dinner together, realizing in mortification that she ought to have attempted to pay her half. *What kind of feminist are you?!* She couldn't remember the last time she'd been out and *hadn't* paid for her half, including her coffee date with Carson Tinsley, which accounted for how infrequently she went anywhere. She had come prepared that night, several weeks of her tips smoothed and tucked into her wristlet.

"But I didn't even offer to pay half the other night and I should ha—"

"Violet." If the commanding rumble of his voice hadn't silenced her, the heat of his hand dropping to her knee would have. "I don't want you to feel that you don't have any agency here. I might be the one giving all the orders, but you hold all the cards. Your comfort is the only thing that counts right now, and if I overstep, I want you to know you can tell me so. But *that's* not happening. Don't think I'm unaware we're at different points in our careers. You can say no, you can say you don't want to see me again, you can tell me to stop coming to the farm when you're working. It's dinner, not a down payment on your time. But I'm in a position to comfortably spoil someone, so when you're with me, I'm spoiling you. End of story."

She *was* a good feminist, she'd told herself, and she definitely couldn't be bought . . . but if he'd have suggested at that moment that he would have appreciated a blow job, she would have fallen face-first on his cock with an open mouth without a shred of hesitation.

Like the previous weekend, the night had ended with a kiss that had nearly turned her inside out, the hot pressure and texture of his tongue reminding her of her suppositions over what it would feel like licking her sex. His giant hand wrapped around her hip, drifting lower as he nibbled on her neck until he palmed her ass, kneading over her cheeks. She could feel the heat of his erection through his neatly tailored trousers, pressing herself tighter, eager for whatever would happen next. *He leaves on a business trip tomorrow and he's missing his milking appointment, he's not going to want to leave town without letting you suck him off at the very least.* She'd been about to ask if they were going back to his place when he released her, locking his hands around her elbows when she swayed.

"I'll miss seeing you this week, but I'll call once I'm back in town."

She'd somehow managed to make it back to her apartment, texting Geillis in aggravation. She appreciated that he was acting like a gentleman and that they were taking a bit of time to get to know one another, she *did*. She was certain if they hadn't that she'd be doubting his interest in her as anything other than a casual human dalliance, her rational mind reminded her of that regularly . . . but the other half of her; the base, animalistic side that thought of nothing but his cock and how it would feel erupting inside her, was ready to climb out of her skin. Her friend's suggestion to her ire had been typical.

Send him nudes.

She'd not had the courage to go that far, but had instead sent a casual photo of herself wearing a thigh-skimming slip of a nightgown, curled atop her blankets. It had taken nearly two hours to set up and artfully arrange herself on the bed in a way that didn't look like a jumble of knobby knees and chubby thighs, taking and discarding photo after photo before she'd sent it off with a message thanking him for dinner, and that she'd miss him while he was gone, opening an incognito tab on her phone to load up some minotaur porn, scrolling until she found a bull with similar coloring to him, and set to work rubbing circles against her aching clit as the human on screen was taken from behind.

* * *

"So you started your business out of spite."

He'd blown out through his wide, pink nostrils, hard enough that it lifted the pecan-brown hair that fell in his face. "That's a tremendous oversimplification."

She'd dissolved into giggles at his wrinkled nose and offended tone, leaning forward in a swoop as she laughed, the solid grip of his hand the only thing that tethered her to the earth until he swung her around to crash into his side, his broad body absorbing her laughter.

"You did too. You took your ball and went home and started your own game."

"A better game," he grumbled in response, earning another peal of laughter from her. "More respectable. Absolutely more profitable."

They were walking along the trail of the town's titular creek several days after he'd returned from his trip, and she'd been asking for the full story on how he'd left his job in the city. He'd started with a company that distributed farm machinery right out of school, working his way up to senior VP of sales, a title that had made her swallow hard. *And you're just happy to have a four-digit bank balance.* She'd learned he'd fled his small-town community as soon as he was able, earning a university scholarship and never looking back. As a result, he wasn't particularly close with the younger siblings he'd left behind. He didn't need to tell her it was something he felt guilty over; she was an expert in guilt and being anxious over other people's feelings, and recognized it when she saw it.

"They stopped caring about the people they were selling to, started cutting corners, going back on their guarantees. At that point the money didn't even matter . . . that could have been my grandfather being taken advantage of, or my brother, or one of the neighbors. I don't ever want to directly work in agriculture again, but they're good people, hard-working people. I like knowing I'm doing my part to help them." He'd shrugged, big hooves clicking on the paved path as they walked. "So I left. Waited out my no-compete clause, rented office space. The people who run this town . . . you only need to get on their good side once. I helped out one of the local farms with a warranty issue on my own time, and that old centaur took my good deed back to the farmer's alliance. By the time I was ready to set up shop, I had all of their business."

Violet gazed up, her heart positively overflowing as he grinned. He was sharp and stoic and unsmiling most of the time, but when he *did* smile it was worth every moment without its light. He was solid where she was anxious, strong when she would have caved, but she thought that her own positivity filled in the gaps of his harder edges; her easier smiles and chipper attitude complimented his steeliness. *Written in the stars.*

"Tell me about the people who run the town," she begged, swinging their joined hands in a most undignified way. "Oh! The Applethorpes, right?" He'd taken her to Applethorpe Manor already, one of Cambric Creek's oldest and grandest residences which had been donated to the town as a museum, and she'd poured over every room; each arch and decorative door transom, every board of the intricate, two-toned herringbone hardwood floor and the meticulously restored wallpaper. It was everything she loved and it thrilled her that he was indulging her interests, and she'd been eager to learn more of the town's apparent checkered history.

"The Applethorpe's," he agreed, "what's left of them, anyway. The Hemmings, obviously, they're at the top of the food chain, and the Irondritchs. Shifters and weres, that's who settled this town originally. I'd love to get you into the Slade manor, we'll have to figure out how to finagle an invite to the Halloween seance. Maybe Lurielle knows someone . . . "

The water widened at that point, spilling over a short cliff of rocks in a spectacular falls view, right in the center of town, and she'd squealed over how picturesque and lovely everything was. Cambric Creek was, she was slightly distressed to learn, just as expensive as the city, if not more so. All of the accommodative architecture and restaurants and scenery came at a cost, one the residents clearly didn't mind paying, and she felt a twinge of guilt over every expensive meal and outing he planned for them, every little gift bag of lace-wrapped artisanal soap and local honey and hand-beaded bracelets she oohed over in shops that she went home with, but he was resolute. Spending time with her was the treat, and the cost of it was meaningless.

If only she knew what to do next. Violet felt stuck in place, a preposterous feeling, considering that she saw him regularly and learned more about what made him tick with each successive week. She adored spending time with him, was ridiculously impressed with his tenacity and ambition, and was turned to goo by his surprising softness with her . . . but he'd paused his visits to the farm, despite her insistence that she didn't want him to do so, and after half a dozen dates and outings with nothing to show for her time—other than a heart that would surely be broken if he were to change his mind—was a pile of dripping panties and a charging cord that had earned a permanent place plugged in beside her bed. She'd been forced to wonder, as she took the much girthier vibrator she'd purchased weeks earlier off said charger, once she'd come home that night—alone, *again*—if his balls were achingly full for all the time they'd spent *not* having sex.

* * *

133

"There we are," Geillis announced cheerfully, after ripping up the last of the wax-smeared papers. "That looks spot on, they really should have let me been more than a shampoo girl, bloody wankers at that place. He'll be able to get his muzzle nice and wet now, you're welcome, luvvie. I expect a bouquet of roses this week, once you've had your kitty licked like a bowl of cream. From both of you. Oh, he can afford the really nice ones too, the long-stemmed jobbies!"

He was coming to the city again the following night, a Thursday, and she was determined there was no way she was letting him deposit her at the building's doorstep without coming upstairs and taking off his pants. *His shirt too. You've never seen him without his shirt on, he might have six nipples.* It wouldn't matter if he did, she thought resolutely. *More to love.*

She needed to figure out what to do next, how to move things along, for she had the niggling suspicion that every time she tilted her chin up expectantly, waiting to be ravished, Rourke was, in fact waiting for her. She needed to stop waffling, stop waiting for things to happen on their own, stop letting the uptight little voice in her head convince her that there was no way he'd be interested in a relationship with someone of her species, of her financial situation, with her at all. Maybe Geillis was right. Maybe she should take off her panties. *Maybe you just shouldn't wear them. Maybe it's time to take this bull by the horns.*

Chapter 14

"Teaching?"

She watched his fork bob back and forth, dancing in the air as he considered the merits of his own question before making its way at last to his mouth, his long eyelashes fluttering closed as he savored the rich chocolate and caramel. Her mother would have had a conniption to see them eating dessert—tuxedo cheesecake, drizzled in caramel and tiramisu—as the starter course, but Violet had discovered over the weeks that his admission of having a sweet tooth was quite serious and that she'd need to acclimate to dessert coming before anything else.

"I make more at Morning Glory," she admitted. She had applied for her substitute teacher's license shortly after graduation, thinking it would be a good way to supplement her job in the urban planning office, but it paid a pittance and she'd quickly remembered just why she'd pursued art history and not art education, as her mother had wanted. "I'm also really terrible with kids, so . . . not the best fit."

He made a strangled noise of revulsion, his face screwing up in disgust before stealing a forkful of her tiramisu. Lurielle's warning had proved prescient, and her dessert choice was never safe from his darting hands. "They'd need to pay a fortune to make that job worth it. Grubby little hands, never listening, I don't blame you."

"No kids for you then?" They'd seen each other barely a dozen times and any conversation about anything more than a month or two in the future was comically wishful thinking on her part—*not really, he's already making plans for next Halloween!*—so it made little sense for her stomach to flip-flop in wait for his answer. *Why are you even asking him, you don't even know if **you** want kids.*

"Now, I didn't say that," he corrected, raising his fork in defense. "I have no doubt in my heart that I'd love my own child with everything in me. Other people's children though, they're . . . they're just terrible." The room they'd been seated in was nearly empty, so there were no other patrons around to give her disapproving looks as she burst out laughing, sliding closer to him on the banquette, seeking his warmth.

Suggesting this restaurant had been by design: she knew they had a fabulous dessert cart that he would love, and there was no traditional seating. Couples would gather on huge velvet poufs and lounged on settees and sat closely together on the long banquettes, as they did then. She was absolutely *not* planning on initiating anything improper while they were seated in the sparsely populated dining room, she only wanted to be nearer to his warmth and press to his side, Violet told herself. If his strong arm were to come around her, so be it. If his thick fingers might stroke her thighs, she'd live. If they somehow made their way under her skirt, discovering her lack of underwear, she was prepared to deal with the consequences.

"Have you ever considered gallery work? Or something in an architecture office?" Finding her a job she would love was his new pet project, networking with his contacts and putting the word out amongst friends. She told herself it was only because he was the type that probably enjoyed a fixer-upper, which she was, but it still liquefied her insides to contemplate. *That doesn't seem like someone who's only interested in a short-term thing, right?*

"The architecture firms want a more specialized degree, and the gallery jobs are all taken by people who don't plan on retiring until after they're dead." He'd wrinkled his nose adorably, nodding his agreement with her sentiment, and she edged closer on the velvet banquette until she was able to feel the heat of his thickly muscled thigh.

It happened midway through dinner.

She had pressed close enough to be flush against him and his arm had dropped around her at last. Violet was certain he was able to feel her heart thumping, could probably smell her arousal over the half-eaten plates of food before them. Her eyes slipped closed, breathing in the warm, woodsy smell of him as his giant hand rubbed the side of her hip, swirling the glass of dark red wine he held in the other. *This is it, this is it.* Violet felt the moment when he realized his fingers weren't moving over any additional fabric beneath the short skirt of her dress, that nothing at all impeded the smooth glide of his fingertips against her hip, no silk or satin or cotton, not even the teensy strap of a thong. She felt him stiffen slightly against her, his hand pausing ever so slightly in its movement before stilling.

False alarm. You'd better buy a backup vibrator now so that when you burn out the first one sometime next week you won't be left with no— Her treacherous inner voice cut off on a gasp, the air in her lungs forced out in a squeak when his velvety touch moved to the inside of her thigh, tracing softly up her skin until he met the resistance of where her thighs met, sealing him out. He stopped moving but hadn't pulled away. *You hold all the cards. Your comfort is the only thing that counts right now.* Her chest was heaving, her breath leaving her in pants. He'd told her explicitly how things were going to work, and she'd been too obstinate to listen. She held all the cards. He'd not continue if she didn't want him to do so. Her thighs parted.

"Violet, do you remember what I told you about what you could expect when you're with me?"

His voice was stern, that of a principal questioning a naughty student; a priest before a sinner, and she gulped.

"You-you said my comfort was all that matters. That I . . . I hold all the cards."

His finger had begun to move back and forth like a clock pendulum, the tip of it just barely grazing her cleft.

"Mhm, exactly. And what else?" Each stroke against her outer lips moved a little easier, a little smoother, aided by her slick against her newly waxed skin. *Geillis is going to get the biggest bouquet of roses they sell.* The velvety-soft digit pressed slightly, breaching her folds and still moving like a pendulum, only now his fingertip pressed into her clit on every pass, a jolt of lightning each time he did so. Her hands fisted in the material of his sleeve, her breath coming out in needy gasps.

"You said . . . you said you were going to spoil me."

"Exactly."

Her mouth dropped open and her head lolled against his arm when the same finger pressed, dipping into her hot folds completely, coating itself in the wetness it found there. When it was joined by one of its brothers—stroking and squeezing, pulling and circling against her clit—she whimpered, and his answering chuckle was so dark and deep she nearly came right then.

"Did you think that meant I wasn't going to spoil this pussy?" His fingers had curled, trapping her clit between his knuckles, stimulating its hidden sides as they locomotored back and forth, pulling back its hood and making her see stars. "You just need to tell me what you want, sweetheart. You're in charge."

Violet didn't feel in charge. She felt as though her spine had suddenly misplaced several vertebrae as she slumped against him, her legs opening a little wider, as though that would somehow help her achieve the friction she craved, the need to come suddenly obliterating everything else. Her clit felt like a live wire, and she was desperate for him to plug her in and make her spark. She didn't see how she was meant to be in charge when *he* was the one playing her body like a musical instrument, laughing that dark chocolate laugh with his CEO voice. *Besides . . . doesn't he know you like him being bossy?*

"You're going to need to tell me what you want, Violet. What does this needy little cunt want from me?" Gruff and commanding, just above her temple, turning her to jelly.

"Please," she whimpered, too aware of the other couple across the dining room and the server slowly making their way around the restaurant; too aware of the way he was rubbing her clit from the top, from the sides, anywhere but where she needed.

"You need to use your words, sweetheart. Please what?"

The outline of his cock stood out in relief in his bespoke grey pants, fat and full and desperate to come out, from the looks of it. She wanted to be filled by his cock, to have him stretch her beyond her limits and fuck her the way he'd fucked her in her dreams a hundred times already, she wanted to feel the way twenty-four ounces would gush out of her . . . but that would have to wait. Right now she couldn't do anything, would never be able to leave this restaurant and see the sun again if she didn't come immediately. He was smiling, she realized. Smiling *that* smile, the one that she loved, and the sparkle in his eye was completely evil. He was a bit of a bastard, but she probably wouldn't have been so hot for him in the first place if he wasn't.

"*Please* make me come. But don't get us arrested," she added hurriedly, glancing guiltily around the room.

The press of his digits had settled into a rhythm by then, cupping her entire mound in his palm, just beneath the jacquard table linens, and she panted when they began rubbing over her clit at last.

"Is this what you need?" His voice was a low croon just above her head, but her eyes had glazed over by then. She was going to come very soon at this rate, orgasming in public, unable to control herself. Who knew what she'd do next in her frenzied state. *I'm sorry, officer, I didn't mean to fellate this minotaur in the middle of the dining room, but you see, he's been playing so fucking hard to get that I snapped.*

"I'll take care of this pretty little pussy anytime you want, sweetheart. Anytime she wants to be licked, I'll be here to lick it and make you come. Eating this pussy is going to be my new favorite meal. Anytime she wants to be stuffed with my fat bull cock, I'll be here to fuck you so good you won't be able to remember your own name. I'm going to spoil you rotten, Violet. I'm going to spoil this cunt every way I can . . . all you need to do is tell me what you need."

She'd wondered, once, if he would say filthy things to her in his stern, always-in-control voice, but she'd never imagine hearing it this way, in a dark croon at her temple. One of his thick fingers pressed into her heat and her legs shot out, kicking at nothing, and Violet understood why some of the minotaurs at the farm shook as if they'd just been struck by lightning when they came. She wasn't sure what was short-circuiting her brain faster—the way he was rubbing her or the things he was saying, but when his finger withdrew, only to re-enter a breath later with a second, she knew she was finished. He fucked into her with a solid, steady pump of his wrist, stroking her inner walls and never letting up the pressure on her clit, and she was nearly embarrassed by how quickly she unspooled under his ministrations, her orgasm building in a tight coil of pressure. When she clenched around him, thighs quivering, he gave a low hum of approval, continuing his movement until her contractions slowed, the pleasurable pulsing of her peak fading away. She watched him through heavy-lidded eyes withdraw his hand and suck his fingers clean, as calm and collected as he ever was, just as the server reappeared to refill the water glasses.

"We might need to make an appearance at the block party, after all, just to put the word out that you're looking for something. Xenna and her brother know everyone in town, if there's something open that might fit the scope of your degree, they'll know it."

His ability to finger fuck her in public and go right back to the conversation about her job prospects without missing a beat was astounding, and she nearly choked on her wine when the server asked if they were enjoying their meal a moment later.

"Do you want to come back to my place?" she mumbled against his arm, once the check had been taken and the table cleared. She'd realized he was too big to force up the stairs, but as long as went willingly on his own, she might be able to lock him inside. *No sense leaving anything to chance.*

His laughter was a rumble against her as he captured her hands in his, leaning down to reach her mouth. She wasn't quite used to the sensation of kissing a mouth so different from her own, one that didn't slot against hers like a puzzle piece, but his lips were unfailingly soft as they pressed to her, soft and insistent.

"Violet, did you really think you were going to come to dinner and tempt me with your bare cunt, let me have a taste of how needy and delicious she is, and then kiss me on the cheek out on the sidewalk and go your merry way?" He enunciated every letter, as sharp and forbidding as he'd been on that very first day, barking that he was on his lunch break. Her nipples tightened and he tsked at her with a shake of his head. "You're making it very hard to be a gentleman, but I think it's time to bring you home."

CHAPTER 14

* * *

She'd never fully appreciated how enormous he was.

In the wide-open milking room where he towered over her on the upper level, there was no accurate scope. When they walked through Cambric Creek or crowded into one of the always-busy little bars or restaurants there, they were surrounded by towering orcs and ogres, trolls and mothmen and small-statured elves and goblins, obliterating her sense of what was normal or not. Here in her apartment, though, he seemed larger than life and completely out of place. *It's alright, it's fine. He's going to find his place right here. Between your legs.*

"You're making it very hard to be a gentleman," he repeated, standing over where she sat on the edge of the bed, thighs parted.

"Is that the only thing that's hard?" Violet gave herself a mental pat herself on the back for continuing their little game, leaning up and pressing her lips to the thick bulge at the front of his pants, slightly above eye-level from where she sat. The solid, steel-cored outline of his cock twitched, and she mewled in need. It had been weeks since she'd handled him at the farm, a veritable *lifetime* since she'd felt his heft and stroked his girth and squeezed his meaty balls, and she felt like she might catch fire if she couldn't take him in hand and run her tongue over his winking slit, feel him stretch her wide and fill her with his hot release.

"Is this what you want?" The bulge at the front of his tailored dress pants twitched again as her fingertips moved to trace over the shape of him, and her palm prickled, needing to feel his weight and thickness.

"Yes," she whispered.

"Yes, what?" Fingertips at her cheek, caressing her jaw.

"*Yes, this is what I want.*" His eyes fluttered shut as she outlined the shape of him, knowing the topography of his member like a map she'd studied for ages, finding one of the veins that snaked up his shaft with ease.

"My cock? Is that what you want, Violet? Do you enjoy stroking my cock at the farm?"

Her mouth ran dry and her legs opened a little wider, vainly seeking friction that wasn't there. Enjoyment didn't even begin to categorize how she felt about having the opportunity to touch him, to stroke him and bring him to release. The velvety pad of his index finger caught her chin, raising her face to his, and all she could do was nod dumbly.

"Words, please." The note of command made her sit up a bit straighter.

"Y-yes," she managed to whisper.

"Yes, what?" He was definitely a bastard, no question. She glared up and his smile stretched, clearly enjoying himself.

"Yes . . . I enjoy stroking your cock. I *love* stroking your cock."

He hummed in approval, a low rumble of thunder against her. "What else do you enjoy?" He made no move to stop her when she dragged down his zipper, his hands assisting by unbuckling his belt.

She loved everything about his milking sessions: the way he grunted when he thrust against the breeding bench with that slow, solid pump of his hips, giving her a delicious hint of what it would be like to have him buried inside her. She loved the hot throb of his testicles when he came and the weight of his cock in her hands, the way his muscles tightened as he emptied because of her.

"The way you throb, and-and the sounds you make. I enjoy milking you dry."

He'd robbed her of the pleasure of his heft as he held his shaft, directing it towards her mouth. The first bump of his cockhead against her lips made her moan, dragging over her lips, and she eagerly opened her mouth, sliding her tongue over him, her jaw popping when he pressed his head in. She wanted to slide her tongue into his sensitive foreskin, wanted to suck on his frenulum and make him groan in pleasure, had just tightened her lips around the flared edge of his big mushroom head, when he pulled away.

"Sweetheart, I'm going to give you this cock so good, you'll never be able to remember anyone else's. . . . but that's not going to happen tonight."

She cried out when he tucked himself away, realizing he had the fucking *audacity* to be serious, whimpering as he did up his fly and rebuckled his belt. The outline of his erection still sat heavily against the fine material of his pants, taunting her, and her fists balled in frustration. "I thought I was in charge? I thought *I* got to call the shots, mister bossy."

His laughter seemed too big for her tiny bedroom, rattling the light fixture and making her breath hitch. "You are sweetheart, and I'm never going to leave you unsatisfied. That's a promise. But I'm not going to do anything that might hurt you, and you're not ready to take my cock. You need to be prepped," he glanced swiftly around the room, nose wrinkling, "and I can barely turn around in here. My hooves will tear up your sheets. You're going to pack a little bag when you come home from work tomorrow and bring it with you on Friday, and spend the weekend at my house. I can't promise you'll be walking right on Monday, but we're going to do things the right way and you won't get hurt."

She might perish before then, she thought miserably, although the cozy little tableau he'd painted bore a striking resemblance to her daydreams—beneath him in his bed, spending time together, screaming in pleasure, snuggling into his warmth. All that was missing was the coffee.

"On your knees, sweetheart. You don't think I'm going to put you to bed without a smile on your face, do you? I already told you, I'm going to spoil your cunt rotten."

It was surreal, being on her hands and knees on the bed, facing the wall, away from the room. She could hear Rourke, could feel the cooler air when he pulled her dress up her back and over her head, breathed out a ragged breath when he cupped her breasts, his breath a hot exhalation on her skin as he rolled her stiffened nipples and slowly caressed his way down her body, but he stayed behind her. She instantly thought of the minotaur porn she'd watched on several occasions by then, the human in the video keeping her eyes closed as her mouth hung open and her head lolled as she was fucked from behind by the huge bull with his coloring.

Rourke's hand came up to meet her center, rubbing wide circles against her lips, finding her sopping. "Violet," he groaned, "you're going to be the death of me."

Just as she had at the restaurant, she fell apart under his ministrations embarrassingly fast. He'd brought a knee up to the bed as he fucked her with two fingers, that same solid thump, and when he added a third, her breath stuttered. He was right, she realized. She would need to work up to the girth of his cock. His ears were just as velvety soft as she'd imagined when she raised her arms to encircle his neck, the bullish snorts of hot air against he skin seeming to set her ablaze as his hand worked against her.

"So beautiful . . ."

She cried out when he pushed her back to her hands and knees, the thump of his own body going to the floor shaking her shelves, and the first licks of his tongue made her spine quiver. His tongue was hot and wide, rougher than a human's, pushing into her and fucking her from behind, a *delicious* sensation she thought would be hard to top, but when it lapped at her clit, her mind went black, leaving nothing behind but golden sparks shooting behind her eyelids.

"I want you to come on my tongue," he ordered in his CEO voice, and just as she'd suspected from the very beginning, she was helpless to obey. "You're always going to come first, sweetheart, always against my mouth, understand?"

She keened as he suckled her clit, feeling the vibrations of her orgasm start in her legs, shaking their way up her thighs until she was spasming, his grip on her hips the only thing keeping her from collapsing into a boneless puddle. She came against his tongue in a wave of convulsions, nearly sobbing when its roughness moved to her opening, pushing inside and drinking her nectar. He continued to lap at her as the throbbing within her slowed, licking her pussy like a man who hadn't eaten in a month, and when his tongue continued its journey against the curve of her skin, never slowing in its vigor as he laved her previously untouched pucker in a mix of his own saliva and her slick, she nearly arched off the bed. *Geillis is going to get every rose in town.*

When he let her drop to the mattress, Violet considered that she might not actually survive the weekend. She'd never had her pussy rubbed as pleasurably, had never been fingered so efficiently before. She'd never, *ever* had her clit licked in a way that nearly made her orgasm immediately, and her ass might never be the same after the tonguing he'd given it. Once he'd prepped her and stretched her; once she'd taken his cock, at last, she'd never be able to come home. She'd never be able to go back to humans, another thing her vampire friend was right about, and she'd never be able to mend her heart if he let it shatter, not once she'd learned if he was as solid and warm in reality as he'd been in her dreams. The wide expanse of his nose huffed against her skin, his lips kissing softly up her back, tracing her spine, until the blanket was drawn over her.

"I'll talk to you tomorrow, sweetheart."

She was barely able to nod as he kissed the top of her head, unable to raise herself from the pillow as she listened to the scrape of his hooves on her floors, the clack of him moving across her tiny kitchen, and the click of her door, signifying he was gone. She liked this new pet name, and she hoped it stuck around. She hoped *he* stuck around. She needed to get up and turn out the light, needed to set the chain and deadbolt in her door, needed to *not* be feeling the Pandora's Box of emotions that were suddenly pressing her to the bed. She couldn't quite account for the tears that were soaking her pillow, and as an inexplicable sob brewed at the back of her throat, the result of this emotional tidal wave, Violet tried to remember to just keep breathing.

Chapter 15

"No coffee tonight," he announced as she entered the collection room, smiling at the way his voice seemed to bounce against the tiles. "We're getting piñata juggernauts. Limited time only. Everybody likes ice cream, you can't say no."

The only camera in the collection room was above the milking machine, and the scope of the fish-eyed lens only captured the machine and the cooler, where the valuable collections were stored. The privacy and anonymity of the clients were one of the farm's top priorities, thus there was no eye in the sky in the top level of the room, leaving her free to climb the short staircase and pull down her mask, stretch up to her toes, and kiss the pink expanse between his exposed nostrils. There was no room for argument or debate, he'd made up his mind and that was final.

Violet tsked, even though she knew that she'd be giving in to his whims. He'd already let her know that he would be hangry and terrible company if they didn't eat something before their last-minute dinner reservation, had been grousing non-stop that it had taken nearly a month to secure and the best time slot offered was at one in the morning. "If they're strolling around getting coffee all day, why can't they have normal reservation times?" he'd demanded the day before, when his name finally came up in the La Vie Rouge reservation queue. She'd be going to his house from work, where she'd wait for him to get home and evidently eat a week's worth of sugar by way of a limited-time iced cream treat. She couldn't wait.

"Okay, first of all, that's very bossy of you. Plus that thing's got to be five thousand calories!"

She'd not anticipated seeing him before then; hadn't expected to see him at the farm at all, but when she'd been handed her files for the day, a purple sticker peeked up from the bottom, setting her heart into a climbing expedition up her throat all afternoon.

Her schedule had been a solid wall of Earners, the easiest day she could have asked for.

"Wait," her first client had ground out, teeth clenching as the nozzle finished him off. "Don't pull it yet, I've got more." Sure enough, after minutes of leg shaking and teeth-gnashing, several more spurts of semen entered the bottle, bringing it just over the fill line. The bull was maybe a decade older than Rourke, sable with ivory markings, with horns filed to smooth, rounded ends and a braided copper ring in his nose. It was an impressive amount, Violet thought as she labeled the bottle, all things considered.

"Our youngest is starting school in the fall," the minotaur said with a shaky laugh, pushing himself off the bench on unsteady legs. "We thought the local university would have been less expensive than moving away, but . . ." He trailed off with a shake of his head and Violet nodded sympathetically.

"Nothing here is inexpensive," she agreed, earning a snort and another nod as the bull hitched up his jeans. "I understand why, and it's such a nice place you wouldn't want to see anything change, but still. It's a lot. You know," she added as the minotaur headed for the door, "oysters and spinach. Add them to your diet, if you're not allergic. The zinc and folate help with, ah, production. If you're trying to bank that first semester . . ." She trailed off with a blush.

"Oysters," he repeated seriously, head bobbing, either not noticing her reddened ears or not caring. "I'll definitely be doing that. Thanks for the tip!"

The rest of the day passed in a similar fashion, and she found herself paying closer attention to her clients than she ever did before. Every minotaur who came in with a ring through his nose left her wondering if he had a new baby at home, a family vacation to save for, a down payment on a house. The bulls without rings may have been students, may have been looking to splurge on a gaming system or pay hospital bills or start building a retirement fund. She'd

147

long ago accepted that Kirime was right: this wasn't sex work, especially not for the employees, but she realized that it likely wasn't for the bulls who visited the farm either. *Humans have commodified us.* This wasn't any different than selling plasma for bar money. She passed the other human in the hall just then, who would forever and always be Stiff Grip Sally in her head, the girl plodding along in a pair of alpine milkmaid scrubs. *Well . . . it's still sexual for some of them.*

She'd practically bounced into the collection room once his file finally rested in her hands, overjoyed that she'd be able to hold him and stroke him again, but he'd yet to release his hold on her as his face screwed up into a familiar pout.

"Then we'll share one," Rourke insisted, dropping his giant hands to her hips, preventing her from pulling away. "You can pick the flavor. There are chocolate stars inside and rainbow confetti, so frankly I don't understand why this is even a conversation. And I'm an eldest child, so just in case you were keeping score, being bossy is *my* birthright."

His always-messy hair tumbled over his forehead, and she leaned forward against him, reaching up to brush it back when she felt it. He was there for his weekly appointment, there to be milked, and he'd always followed the courtesies of the farm. It was preposterous for the heavy bulge at the front of his pants to shock her, but she gasped all the same when he pulled her flush against him, a slow, closed mouth grin spreading across his face. She'd held his cock in her hands, had stroked and pumped it, knew its weight and sensitivities . . . but feeling it pressed to her, even through several layers of clothing, when she'd not yet felt it *pressed* to her was tortuous. She clawed at his broad chest for purchase, whimpering when his hips shifted, moving the hard bulge against her.

"You know," he murmured, hands continuing to press her to him, "I was originally going to cancel today. I've got a hot date tonight, figured I should probably stay home and get ready. Then I thought it might be smart to keep my normal appointment, take the edge off before tonight . . . but now I think I'd rather keep the edge. Save it all for her."

"Oh?" her voice came out on a squeak, and his smile twitched. "And what made you change your mind?"

"Well, you know, I like this girl. A lot. We have a great connection, we have fun together. I can envision her in my life in five years, ten years. And I know that probably seems a bit premature, moving a little fast, but this isn't my first rodeo and I've been stupid in relationships before. Now I know what I want, and she checks all my boxes. I think I do for her as well. And tonight is supposed to be the big night. We've been taking things slow, I'm a gentleman after all . . ."

Her throat closed and her finger clenched the material of his crisp dress shirt, a shade of lavender that was so pale it was nearly silver. If he'd rushed her into bed as quickly as she would have liked, she would always wonder if that's all their relationship was to him—sexual release from a source he already knew could satisfy him. He liked her *personal touch*, and she'd always be insecure that was all she was to him. It was backward thinking and stupidly outdated, but her mother and aunt had talked about *no one buying the cow when the milk is free* for years, and she'd obviously absorbed a bit of it.

Instead, he'd brought her into his life and had given her the opportunity to call the shots. *He's been making such an effort, literally from day one.* He'd picked most of their date locales, he'd taken a step away from her work to prevent muddying the waters. They'd been hiking and had gone for walks in the park, she had seen grand old buildings and beautiful art, tried new food and met his neighbor and obvious friend. He'd acknowledged their different social standings and had given her every opportunity to change her mind . . . like a gentleman. Her cheeks colored when she realized how little sex actually had to do with it.

"Like a perfect gentleman," she agreed, leaning into him. Nothing was said for a long moment, and he cradled the side of her face in his palm, what had become a familiar, tender gesture. The pressure of his velvet thumb against her cheek was a whisper, and she thought he was right: he checked all her boxes.

His smile lit the room, and she swayed. "I'm going to leave. Save this all for later." Back and forth, a movement so slow she might have thought she was imagining it, he pressed his erection against her, a promise, she thought, of things to come. It wasn't all about sex, but the sex was absolutely going to be a perk. *It's a good thing we're going back to his place then. You'd wind up gumming up the washing machine in the building from the mess on the sheets. Mrs. Muehlstein will try to do her laundry after you and get everything covered in minotaur milk.* "As a matter of fact," he continued, interrupting himself with a slight groan when she twisted her hips to grind into the bulge in his pants, "I'm not even sure we're going to make it to get ice cream. We might need to jump right to the post-dessert activities."

"That'll just make the main course more satisfying," she suggested with a laugh, pushing herself off his chest until he released her hips. As much as she wanted to drop to her knees and service him with her mouth right there, it wouldn't do to get caught, not if she wanted to still be employed tomorrow, and she was forced to agree with him—keeping an edge had been thrilling, if not a teensy weensy bit frustrating.

"I guess I should get going if I'm not giving a collection today. I might end up surprising my date early. I hope she comes prepared."

* * *

She thought he might have been joking.

His massive truck was sitting in the driveway when she pulled up to the address he'd given her—a cute little cape cod-style on a tree-lined street—and she half expected him to be waiting at the door, ready to lead her on to the night's adventures. Instead, she'd needed to knock, letting herself in when his deep voice bellowed that it was unlocked from somewhere deep in the house.

Her earlier explorations of the neighborhoods in Cambric Creek had not gone amiss, for she saw immediately that the entire house seemed designed for someone his size. Rourke's slate blue house was nestled in between two of identical build, the accommodative architecture that made this multi-species community so in-demand. The doorways were wide and tall, the depth between the counters and the cupboards great enough that his horns would be safe from collision, everything bigger, taller, designed for someone of stature and bulk.

She'd just stepped through the kitchen, eyeing the green tartan blanket on the back of the sofa when he appeared.

The small, white towel, slung low across his hips was all that he wore. *Wore* was a bit of an overstatement, she realized, for the jut of his erection pushed forward the front of the towel, showing the curve of his heavy balls just beneath the hem. Dragging her eyes up his taut abdomen, over his pebbled nipples and broad shoulders, taking in the way his short hide thickened around his neck, full and plush, she wanted nothing more than to wake up beside him with her face pressed to his throat. Her eyes continued their hungry climb, landing at last on his aggrieved scowl.

"You're wearing entirely too many clothes."

"I thought we were going for ice cream!" she exclaimed with a laugh, earning a terse head shake in return.

He tsked, crossing his massive arms over his chest, and she held her breath, but the towel stayed where it was. "We discussed this. After-dessert activities first. *Then* dessert. Then we'll need to take a nap since we're going to dinner in the middle of the fucking night."

The dress she'd be wearing to the restaurant that night belonged to Geillis: a black dress more sophisticated than anything else she owned, with a deep, plunging center, cut down to the small of her back and the middle of her chest respectively, making an ordinary bra an impossibility, but she should have known that borrowing anything from Geillis would automatically mean that ordinary would not be a part of the equation.

"The goal is to show some skin, not cover up like a bloody abbess! Of *course* you're not going to wear a bra, do you want him to be able to reach across the table and pinch your nipple or not?!"

The thought of Rourke nonchalantly freeing her breast at the dinner table to play with her nipples in front of the other patrons was a preposterous one, but she would have been a liar if she'd claimed it hadn't made her wet. The dress was safely secured in her backseat, and she'd chosen a simple sleeveless shift for the start of the evening's adventures, appropriate for getting ice cream and strolling through town, or whatever else she thought he might have had up his sleeve.

"This needs to go. Immediately."

She had barely enough time to kick off her shoes before he was drawing the zipper down her back, letting it puddle around her ankles, his scowl growing deeper as he eyed her mesh bra and panties. "I can't believe you wore underwear! *Now* you want to keep your panties on. Violet, did you by chance think I was talking about a *different* date?"

He continued to glower as she laughed, but made no move to stop her when she reached out and tugged on the corner of the towel, letting it fall to the floor, freeing his cock with a bounce. Full and fat and completely delicious, and hers for the taking. "If there's someone else coming, she's going to need to get in line, I've waited long enough." His eyes closed with a groan when she wrapped her hand around his stiff shaft, stroking it as she'd done countless times before, knowing exactly how he liked to be touched.

"Is this what you want, sweetheart? Is this cock what you want?"

She continued to stroke him as he walked them backward down the hallway, turning her to drop onto her back against the biggest bed she'd ever seen. She was struck at that moment, gazing up at him, at how completely non-human he really was. It was an easy thing to overlook at the farm: minotaurs came and went in a constant stream all day long, and she never saw more of them than the view afforded by the milking room's lower level, from their hips up. Clad in t-shirts and uniforms and business attire, it was easy to trick herself that under their clothes, they would look like any other human, if not bulkier. Seeing him like this, standing over her—broad-chested and thick with muscle, every inch of him covered in his silky-coarse hide, his bulging thighs giving way to hocks and hooves, his thin tail a sinuous whip behind him—felt positively primal. *Definitely no going back to humans after this.* "This is the *only* cock I want. I feel like I'm an Athenian sacrifice."

His responding chuckle was a rumble against her breasts as he covered her. "You know what happened to those sacrifices, right? What did they teach you in your human schools? That the minotaur ate all of the tributes? That's true, but not the way you think. I'm going to give you this cock, sweetheart . . .

but you know the rules. First, you need to come on my tongue, or nothing else happens."

His tumble of messy hair tickled her stomach as he kissed his way down her body, pausing to press his wide nose to the front of her panties. The heat of his mouth closed over the gusset, the press of his tongue against the material—wide and hot, *so hot*—scraped over her clit and she arched. Being sucked through the mesh of her underwear shouldn't have been as hot as it was, Violet thought, but when he abruptly changed direction, moving back up her body to her mouth, she yelped in dismay, grabbing onto his shoulders as his huge horns loomed above her.

"Violet, I just wanted to say . . . I really like you." The sharp tone was gone, his commanding CEO voice replaced with a ring of sincerity. "I'm glad we took some time to get to know each other. I know this wasn't exactly a traditional way to meet, and I wanted to make sure you knew I was interested in *you*. Not just your perfect, tiny hands."

Her indignant laugh cut off of a gasp as his mouth met hers, teeth pulling her lip. She liked him too, liked him enough that she could see herself in a relationship with him, could more than imagine those lazy Sunday mornings, the coffee and snuggling and soft lovemaking. He was more than just a client at the clinic, more than initials and an ID number on a white-filled bottle.

The heat of his tongue was like a trail of fire, laving at each of her nipples in turn, catching them in his blunt teeth, scraping and snuffling, breathing his molten heat across her stomach and over her hips. When his wide muzzle nosed against her thighs, her legs fell open once more, gladly allowing him to press against her, his thick tongue pressing into her folds. She wasn't sure if the time would come when she wouldn't completely fall apart as he ate her, completely engulfing her entire sex with his huge mouth. His tongue was so thick and wide that it moved across every inch of her, from clit to slit, and it was the all-consuming pressure and heat and his *impeccable* sense of rhythm that pushed her over the edge. The shape of his mouth meant he didn't so much suck on her clit as he did slurp on it, an act that involved the roughness of his tongue and the pressure of suction, but wetter and somehow *so much* better, better than anything she'd ever experienced before and likely never would again. The pressure that began mounting behind her navel began to involve her legs, a twitching convulsion that involved her entire nervous system as he slurped at her clit, groaning encouragement that sent her to the stars. Her hands locked around his horns as she shook, cunt throbbing against the roughness of his tongue, and the bastard had the nerve to laugh, the vibrations of his chuckle against her making her contort all over again.

When he coated his thick fingers in a lube retrieved from the bedside table, the smell immediately made her sit up. "Did you get that from the farm?!"

"Actually, I did. It came in my third reward tier."

"Your *what*? Wait, never mind, tell me later. Use a little bit more, it feels thick but it loosens up the more you work it." She dropped back on the mattress again, breathing deeply. She could do this. *You just need to relax, don't tighten anything up.*

His first finger stroked into her slowly, pressing into her walls and curling in all the right places. It was a slow, delicious torture. His second finger added a fullness to the pleasure, and he continued to press and stretch, scissoring them open against her resistance, and Violet knew she was meant to be focused on opening up for him, but it felt so ridiculously good that she moaned, earning a reproachful huff. The third was a much tighter fit, and she was reminded that his hands were considerably larger than those belonging to his human counterparts.

"I'm going to go slow, but I want you to tell me if it's too much." A deep rumble that brokered no argument, her eyes fluttering as his hand continued to move. Watching him drizzle the viscous lubricant over his cock was more erotic than it had the right to be, and then he was dragging the fist-sized head over her clit and her composure broke.

"Please," she whimpered, "please please please . . . I need your cock so bad." Her begging broke on a gasp as the thick flare of his head caught at her lips when he pressed into her, agonizingly slow. In the morning she might look back with rose-colored glasses, might remember nothing but the pleasure, but at that moment she felt the burn, his fat cock stretching her further than she'd ever been stretched, pressing into her steadily.

"You don't need to beg for it, Violet, it's yours, anytime you want it. I'm going to spoil your pussy with this big bull cock every day if that's what you want."

The backward drag of him pulling out made her throat stick, and then he was pushing back in, further than he'd gone before, and Violet was positive she felt it pressing into her spine. "Yes, give it to me," she wheezed, burying her fingers into the thicker hide around his shoulders as he began to pump. Slow and deep, deeper than she'd ever been fucked, and it was *so fucking good.* "You've been so good," she babbled, "so sweet and bossy and I love it and you're such a gentleman and I love your cock." His hands slipped under her ass as he groaned, tilting her hips in a way that made her wheeze.

"There's nothing gentlemanly about the way I'm going to fuck you, sweetheart."

She felt a pressure at her entrance, uncomfortable with a slight burn and she had no idea what it could possibly be . . . he grunted as he thrust, a white-hot pain ripping through her and she realized it was the thick swell of his shaft that all the bulls at the farm possessed. Too much, too much . . . *you weren't even taking half of him and it felt like the biggest thing in the world.* Once . . .twice. . . a slight shift of her hips . . . and on the third pump of his hips she moaned, the pain replaced with a pleasure that wiped her vision.

When he pulled out, she thought she might scream. Her face pressed to the bed when he flipped her, his oddly-angled hips pressing into her from behind. "Do you know what happened to the tributes in the labyrinth, Violet?" The swollen, streaming head of his cock pressed into her on a much smoother glide than it had the first time, dragging against her and stretching her wide, making her pant. "They were given to the minotaur to appease his lust. His insatiable lust, that no human man could match."

The stretch of his swell, still a burn, a deeper pressure, and then he groaned, bottoming out in her at last. She'd never before been so full, so stuffed, and she was sure the outline of his cock would be visible through her belly, were she not still face down on the bed.

"They had to send new tributes every year, but the old ones never left. They stayed because they were addicted to the way they were filled," his hips gripped hers, drawing back slowly, "addicted to the way they were fucked by the bull." A firm thrust, and then a second, the same solid, steady pounding she'd imagined as he thrust against the bench. With every slam of his hips, she felt his hide-covered skin and bulging thighs, could well imagine the way his wide hooves scraped against the flooring as he rutted her slowly, feeling every inch a tribute to the minotaur, completely addicted to the way he was fucking her. When his heavy balls began to slap against her, she unraveled.

"I want to feel you come around my cock, Violet. I want you to squeeze me until your cunt has the permanent shape of me, because it's the only cock that's ever going to make you scream like this again." His thrusts into her began to take on a sense of urgency as she babbled, grunting as his cock kissed the most sensitive spots inside her, pounding into her the same way he'd fucked into her hands at the farm. He'd missed his milking, had missed the opportunity to take the edge off his arousal, and tomorrow they could spend all day with soft lovemaking. She could do nothing to provide a plentiful speedy collection from where she was pinned beneath him, but her bull needed milking, and she was desperate to help him over the edge.

"Come inside me," she begged, her legs beginning to shake. The drag of his cockhead against her g-spot was making her stomach seize, and the stretch of that swell had her nearly sobbing in pleasure. "Please please, empty those big balls inside me, I want you to give me every drop."

When his thick fingers began to stroke circles around her clit, she was finished. His neighbors probably thought someone was being murdered, but she was unable to control the strangled wail that ripped from her throat as her pussy clenched, tears running down her cheeks at how good it was. The first burst within her was a molten wave, the roar of his moan making the room shake as he came. Pulse after pulse of heat, those big balls throbbing, and through it all, he never stopped pumping. She knew how much he came, saw the evidence of his orgasms every week, but nothing had prepared her for being on the receiving end of twenty-four ounces of his hot milk. She was able to feel it already dripping out of her, the obscene squelch of his erupting cock emphasizing the mess that was being made. One last groan, one last hot spurt inside of her, and he was done, slumping against the elbows he'd braced around her so that she'd not be crushed under his weight.

This is it, she thought. *He'd better be in this for the long haul because he's ruined you for any other cock.*

The withdrawal was a stomach-quivering absence of pressure, followed by a *gush* of fluid that nearly made her come again.

"Fuck. This is a waterproof blanket, but I should have put down a few towels," he groaned. Instantly, his hands were everywhere: stroking her back, her hips, her hair, wrapping around her middle and gently pulling her flush to him. "Violet, are you okay? I didn't hurt you, did I? Talk to me sweetheart, I need to hear your words. Am I going to need to carry you to get ice cream?"

She laughed. Violet couldn't help herself. It started in her toes and reverberated up her body, coming out of her mouth in a peal of colored light, utterly absent of stress or worry. He was sharp and charming and ridiculously bossy, and she thought she might already be half in love with him. She was thoroughly fucked, and they were about to get ice cream for early dinner. "You really are such a gentleman."

First, though, she had to get up. Get up and clean up, which might be quite the undertaking, covered as she was in his sticky, sweet cream.

VI

HEA

Three Months Later . . .

Chapter 16

T he sunlight pouring through the open shade was cutting.

Violet groaned, shifting against the bunched sheets before snuggling against the broad chest beneath her cheek, squinting against the light. Rourke snuffled and huffed, the muscular arm around her tensing for a moment before he relaxed once more, his deep breaths resuming.

Saturday mornings were for lazing, sleeping off the previous night's physical exertions before embarking on weekend adventures, and this—nestled against his warm skin, with a leg over his thickly muscled thigh and his heavy cock pressed to her front, his strong arm wrapped around her back—had become her favorite place to be. She'd never been the type to laze in bed, not previously. Too many years of early classes, of TA duties and tutoring sessions and work commutes; too many responsibilities that had her up before the sun on most days. Still being in bed this late in the morning would have been a cause for panic to her then, but then again, she'd never previously experienced the joy of falling directly into bed with an eager partner as soon as she walked through the door on Friday evening, followed by a dessert as large as her head.

Despite the previous night's activities, there were things she wanted to do today. Cambric Creek, she'd discovered, was full of interesting little diversions for a couple to enjoy hand-in-hand—botanical gardens, interesting galleries, an old-fashioned observatory, and the picturesque little town square—and she had enjoyed discovering them all over the last several months. Summertime had meant street fairs and shopping, concerts in the park and community carnivals, followed by sharing an extra-late dinner before returning to the sanctuary and pleasure of his giant bed. Now that the summer months were waning, the shops around town had already begun to transition to their autumn displays, and she was excited to see what fun things would be on the community calendar.

"It's time to get up," she groaned, running her palm down his chest, scratching his solid stomach. Rourke grunted but made no movement. "Common, don't be lazy. We wanted to go to the flower shop's plant sale, remember?" She'd already picked out a large rubber tree to place by the sunny window in his living room, a ficus for the kitchen, and a small tray of succulents for her apartment's tiny window ledge, but getting out of bed would be a necessary prerequisite to procuring anything.

The little shop was run by three identical sisters, each with glossy black hair and beetle-like bodies of iridescent green, who collectively seemed to know everything one could about houseplants. She'd been lured in one sunny Sunday afternoon, entranced by the vivid colors of the stained glass window display, pulling Rourke by the hand. The sisters had converged around her, cooing how nice it was to have a human stop in, and would she be interested in seeing one of their home-cultivated pitcher plants?

On the other side of the flower shop was an occultist's tea room, a narrow space where Rourke's wide shoulders and wider horns had been hilariously out of place the first time she'd dragged him in for lunch. Beside the tea room was a small salon which specialized in "cub cuts," as evidenced by the small, fuzzy worgen and gnoll children whom she'd watched through the window as they zoomed in circles around the harried-looking stylists, and she'd wondered, not for the first time, what her own mixed-species offspring might look like. *Not for a decade. At least.*

"You need to make a friend," he'd grumbled good-naturedly that day she'd left the tea room together. "And we need to go get *real* food now because those sandwiches were for children. Pixie children."

Yes, Cambric Creek was full of strange and interesting things: new discoveries she made nearly every week at her boyfriend's side, and warm and friendly residents who didn't seem to care that she was a human. Despite the other species who lived in Bridgeton, humans were still the default majority and mixed-species couples were unusual. Violet couldn't help but notice the looks she occasionally garnered in her own neighborhood when Rourke came to her, sidelong glances she never experienced when she stayed with him. She had begun to dread Sunday evenings when she would leave the quirky little town and his side, her apartment in the city too empty and no longer feeling like home.

"Moonstone!" she whined into his skin, huffing when he ignored her. Any other morning she might have snuggled back against his warm side and let sleep claim her, more comfortable in his arms than she was in any other place on earth, but today she was wide awake, the mid-week appointment on her phone's calendar already spiking her anxiety. She wanted to buy her plants and get her coffee and be distracted by him and the town, and try not to think about how nervous she was.

The short, coarse hair that covered his skin was smooth beneath her palm as she ran a hand down his chest, stroking over his taut abdomen. He was thick with muscle, solid beneath her, the warmth of him increasing the closer her hand drifted to his groin. When she palmed the familiar weight of his cock, squeezing lightly before her fingertips drifted lower to graze his heavy testicles, he grunted into the pillow, shifting slightly. It didn't make a difference how tired he might claim to be . . . there was one sure way to wake him up.

Massive in her hand and impossibly thick, even in its softened state, his cock was a comfortably familiar weight as she dragged her fingers slowly up his shaft and down again, encouraging his foreskin to slide with the motion, gradually exposing his pink head. A tiny bead of moisture pooled in the slit, visible every time she exposed the shiny glans, too delectable to resist wanting to taste it on her tongue. A deep rumble emitted from his chest as she kissed her way down its broad expanse, slowing over his stomach. By the time her lips had reached the crease of this muscled thigh, his cock had stiffened enough that she was able to grip the shaft, leading it to her outstretched tongue.

It was a waste, a terrible, awful waste, bottling his potent release and sending it off to be refined into little blue pills for human men. Now that she knew how sweet it was on her tongue, how *good* it felt to be filled until it ran down her thighs and made a mess of the towels upon the sheets, she hated the idea of him selling it. Her tongue pressed into the slit on his head, lapping up the beading precome before sliding into the edge of his foreskin. She'd perfected the art of maneuvering her tongue into the nerve-ending-packed sheath, sliding around his cockhead from within, licking the inside of his foreskin and tugging it gently with her teeth, as she did then.

"What are you trying to do to me," he groaned, his giant hand landing on the back of her head, thick fingers threading through her hair as she bobbed shallowly on his length, sleep forgotten, and she smiled around him in satisfaction.

He was too big to suck properly. She'd tried, more than once, determined to mimic the abilities of the woman in videos and the countless other women whom she was sure would have been happy to take her place, but all that she'd managed to do was make herself gag on less than a third of his prodigious length.

"St-stop! *Hugghhh . . . "*

She'd pulled back in surprise from where she'd knelt before him, months earlier, a thin strand of drool connecting her mouth to his cock, only to watch her giant, strong boyfriend retch dramatically. "I can't—I can't deal with gagging," he gasped, hunching nearly to where she knelt before him, horns cutting through the air. "*Hurgghh . . .*you gag, I gag. Don't-don't do that again. If I wanted a deep throat that badly, I'd buy one of those milking machines."

She'd wound up curled in a ball on the floor, wheezing with laughter at his feet before he'd controlled his gag reflex enough to scoop her up with a growl, bouncing her down in the center of his giant bed and forcing his mouth between her legs.

Since then she'd perfected her alternate routine of licking and sucking on his bulbous cockhead, stroking him in the way she already knew he enjoyed and mouthing at his heavy sack. Rourke groaned as she worked his foreskin back, sucking his head into her mouth as her hands squeezed and stroked. A stack of towels now lived on the bedside table beside the pump-sized bottle of lube, just within reach, and she snagged one then, depressing a dollop of the clear, viscous gel into her palm. Despite the copious amount of semen she collected from him each week at the farm, weekend morning yields, after passion-filled nights, were considerably less impressive. Enough to necessitate a towel, but not enough to need three.

"You really want those damned plants," he groaned, tightening his hand in her hair as she sucked harder. Her job at the farm necessitated short, well-kept nails, and in the last several months, she'd discovered another perk to the low-frills manicure as she coated her fingers in the thick lubricant. It was

165

a juggling act—keeping her mouth around his cock and milking his balls with one hand, while using the other to work two fingers into his ass, the tight ring of muscle sucking her in as she pumped against him, seeking his sweet spot—but it never failed to make him erupt like a geyser.

She remembered wondering if he would always be so uptight and controlled, or if he would grace her ears with a full-throated moan of pleasure in the privacy of his own bed. She'd long ago received her answer, and his deep bellow rattled the walls as his orgasm hit. When the first burst of his thick cream hit her throat, she swallowed greedily, endeavoring not to choke as her mouth was filled. The towel came in handy to catch the overflow as his balls throbbed in her hand, spurt after spurt until he sagged, his spent cock slipping from her lips.

There were two hampers in the bathroom—one for daily use, and one for the cleanup towels that were washed separately with a special enzyme, several pods of which she'd brought home, just in case, thinking of Mrs. Muehlstein and the sanctity of her cardigans. Towels cleared, hands cleaned, and then she was back in the bed, climbing up his body and collapsing against his heat.

"It's time to get up," she whispered against his throat, nuzzling into the thick hair there, arching against the hand he stroked down her spine. His wide, pink nose pressed to her hair, agreeing with a grunt when a deep, lushly-accented voice broke the quiet of the room.

"Junie, do not—do *not* even think of it. Get back over—Junie!"

The high-pitched yip of Rourke's neighbor's little dog rose in volume and the man's voice took on a desperate tone. Rourke snorted and she managed to stifle her giggle as the man's voice beseeched the dog. "Junie, *please* . . . you're gonna wake up Mama, and then we'll both be in trouble. Is that what you want?" The dog continued to yip shrilly as if that was exactly what she wanted, and Violet was unable to hold back her laughter then, climbing from the bed, pulling Rourke's hand to follow.

By the time they were both dressed and ready to leave the house, the small terror known as Junie had been re-corralled in her own yard. Lurielle stood barefoot in the grass, her thick thighs and full bottom encased in a pair of tiny, terrycloth shorts and t-shirt with the logo of the local observatory emblazoned across it. A few yards away, Khash knelt, his own generous ass in the air as she gave instruction on where exactly she wanted him to dig a hole for the mum plants sitting on the patio's edge. When she saw Violet, the elf waved brightly.

"Well?" she demanded. "How did it go?"

"The video call was this week," Violet began, feeling her pulse kick up at just the thought, "and they called me back for a face-to-face. I meet with the director of development this week."

"Perfect," the elf crowed. "They're going to love you! Just remember, they're all about the community angle, the legacy of the town and their name, blah blah blah. Don't undersell that end of it."

"I won't," she agreed, thinking she'd not even need to exaggerate. She increasingly couldn't see herself staying in the city much longer, couldn't stand living so far from both the farm and Rourke. She was eager to call Cambric Creek home, and if she got this job, it would have to become a reality.

* * *

In the end, it had been Lurielle's friend Dynah's lead. Dynah was a petite, purple-skinned elf with a billow of auburn hair, a nervous, high-pitched laugh, and the ability to talk for ten minutes at a time without taking a breath. She lived next door to a witch who worked in the local hospital; the witch was friends with a home health aid who happened to have the inside track on the Slade Foundation's upcoming initiatives for the new year, including their hiring needs.

The job would be perfect.

It was largely a research position, digging into archives to recreate the textiles and paint colors of some of the grandest buildings in town; full-time, and right there in Cambric Creek. The office she'd be working out of was in a former caretaker's cottage that was grander than any house she'd ever lived in, within walking distance to the Black Sheep Beanery and the other shops and restaurants on Main Street. The pay was commensurate with what she made at the farm, and the flexibility of the tiny office meant she'd still be able to keep several shifts a week there.

Violet was half certain it was an elaborate joke, for dreamy-sounding jobs in cozy little carriage houses with ivy-clad walls in quaint little towns only existed in those predictable romance movies that she would binge watch from her sofa. *You're going to hate your co-worker, but then you'll be paired together to create a wallpaper-making contest for the whole town that everyone will be really excited over, and then you'll inevitably fall in love.* The only problem with that network-ready scenario was the minotaur waiting for her to call him, whose bossiness she loved and whose cock she'd determined she simply couldn't live without. *Sorry, wallpaper boy. It's not gonna work out. I already have a gentleman at home.*

* * *

"Do you want me to quit?" she asked him later that night, once she was nestled against him in bed.

"Wait, what?" he demanded, his wide brow furrowing. "Why? No, of course not. What kind of grade A shit would I have to be to insist that you quit the job where I met you? Do *you* want to quit? That's your choice, sweetheart, you know I'll support whatever you want to do. It's not terrible working conditions, is it?"

"No," she'd quickly assured him. "No, of course not. I really like it there, everyone is really nice. I love the other techs. And you know, the guys who are too into it are actually pretty far and few between when you tally up the days. I don't actually want to leave . . . I just want to make sure you're still okay with it."

His brow had furrowed again, and Violet found herself explaining the difference between clients like him, the Clockwatchers, and the Earners, and the Good Little Cows.

"The *what?!*" His laughter was an earthquake, quickly turning to disgust.

and then laughter again, dislodging her from his side to get up on hands and knees and demand that she "milk him like one of her French cows."

She would keep the two shifts a week at the farm if she did get this job, she'd decided. The extra income could be earmarked exclusively for paying down her highest interest credit card, leaving more of her salary to go towards her loans . . . and besides, she hated the idea of any other technician handling her bull.

"It's going to be fine, Violet." Tucked against his chest was the safest place in the world to be, enveloped in his heat with the thud of his heartbeat under her ear. His deep voice rolled over her like a wave, divining her anxiety without her needing to say a word. There was a unit in Geillis's building, soon available, a small miracle if she actually got this job, and unlikely to stay vacant for long if she waffled. She needed to decide what to do very soon, and the weight of everything—the interview and the bubble of hope within her, the apartment, the thought of having to pack and move, the conversation she'd need to have with her mother—it was all too much. "It will all work out."

"But what if it doesn't?" she whispered, unable to keep the wolves of her thoughts at bay. "I'm not good at making big decisions." The weight of his hand at her back kept her grounded, a stroking pressure at her skin, pushing the wolves away.

"Well, good news, sweetheart. I am. It's going to be fine . . . get some sleep. You've got a big week."

* * *

The smell of coffee seemed to seep into her bones.

Violet took a deep breath, trying to center herself and banish her nerves. *There's nothing to worry about, this will be great. Like he said, everything's going to work out.* She'd arrived too early, as usual, anxious at the thought of hitting traffic and being late; preferring to be safe rather than sorry. It was a baseless fear, for she'd been making this drive five days a week for months now and traffic was usually minimal at this hour. All her extra caution had done was give her ample time to twist herself into knots, trying to remember why exactly why she would be a good fit for the Slade Foundation, trying to remember her qualifications, her degree study, her name.

She'd started the day putting into effect an old trick from her university days: pack as much trauma into a single twenty-four-hour period and save the rest of the week for the outcome. She was nervous over the call home she needed to make, nervous over her interview that afternoon . . . best combine the two and get it over with.

"Oh, I'm so glad you called, pumpkin! Did you get a chance to call Mrs. Murphy at the museum? I think this is going to be such a good opportunity for you, and just think! You'll be able to move home!"

Violet grit her teeth, sucking in a slow breath. Her mother had called the previous week, leaving her a long message about her friend at the art museum in the neighboring suburb of the human town where she'd grown up. Mrs. Murphy was looking to fill three docent positions, and her mother had practically already signed Violet up for one of them, regardless of whether it had anything to do with her very expensive master's degree.

"I know this is probably a bit under your level, darling, but you have to think about getting a foot in the door somewhere!" The museum in question focused largely on modern and contemporary art, as far away from her discipline as one could get and still be in the same building.

"I didn't, mom, I'm sorry. That's not something I'm interested in, to be honest. Those jobs are usually part-time, so that's not really going to help with my bills . . . anyway, I'm calling with good news! I have an interview this afternoon for my exact specialty, and it's not in the city."

Her mother paused, and Violet could practically hear her mentally warring with the desire to be supportive and her feelings of being slighted. "Oh, well . . . I suppose that is good news, dear. Not in the city? Does that mean you might be moving closer to home?"

Here goes nothing. Deep breath. "No, unfortunately. It's in a suburb of Bridgeton, it's the same town I've been working in, so I could technically keep my apartment, but I don't think I'm going to. It's so nice, I really love it here."

She listened to her mother make a series of small noises as she steeled her nerves. "And it's where my boyfriend lives, so I'm probably not going to be staying in the city much longer."

Over the course of her slow courtship, she had joined several online groups for interspecies couples, and the women there waxed poetic about their relationships, with only the occasional complaint about culture clashes or in-law awkwardness. Lurielle had been far more honest, and she'd appreciated the elf's bluntness more than she'd been able to express.

"It's mostly good . . . but sometimes it fucking sucks," she'd said with a shrug, topping off the wine glass before her. Lurielle's boyfriend was one of the swooniest orcs Violet had ever seen, a towering, sticky-voiced southern gentleman who had an anecdote for every situation, who'd nearly turned yellow when she told the group about her burgeoning student loans, earnestly offering to look over her repayment agreements free of charge to find a hidden loophole that would decrease her amounts owed.

"And if you ever need anything, darlin', I'm over in the Templeton, right across the river." The Templeton was one of the poshest high rises in the city, and if her imposter syndrome hadn't already had her feeling like a pauper at the table full of professionals, between Rourke and the couple next door, the notion of just swinging across the river with her gas station coffee certainly would have.

"Like, super sucks. And it's always just the little things, you know? Little things, cultural things that come up that you don't think will be a big deal but then they are, because neither of you wants to compromise, because it doesn't *seem* like it should be a big deal." Violet had nodded, at rapt attention as the elf sipped from her glass before continuing. "People will say things, usually nothing overt, but little comments that are just enough to sting. It's weird, living here you become so insulated from all that . . . like, there's a reason the housing market here is so hot, and people don't *ever* leave. That's why I bought this house knowing I'd be stuck living with a stepladder in every room."

She'd given Violet a tour of her own home that evening, a mirror image of

171

Rourke's, designed for a much larger species like his, painted a sunny yellow. "It was all that was available in my price range at the time. I was moving here for a job so I needed to live somewhere, and the agent said it's sometimes months before things hit the market. I had planned on remodeling this year . . . and it worked out that I don't need to. Now he reaches everything on the shelves and I don't have to balance on ladders just to put away the dishes."

"The schools are great, the community is really inclusive and busy . . . you forget what it's like in other places."

"I've already noticed, " Violet had blurted, nodding vehemently. "You know I live in the city. Every time he comes to me, whenever we're out there will always be at least one person who stares. I think it's the tail. And it's almost always another human," she added with a grimace.

"Not always," Lurielle had grumbled. "Khash lives in the city too. We were at the grocery store near his apartment and this little old bat woman asked if we were planning on adopting because I'd never be able to carry an orc." She scowled at the memory before tipping back her glass. "Considering I had a pregnancy test on the conveyor belt . . . let's just say I didn't take it well."

Violet had swallowed, desperately wanting to ask how the huge orc didn't split the petite elf in half every time they had sex. "Are—are you . . .?"

"I'm not, thank the goddess. We're smart people who are both bad at birth control, so every month is an adventure. Anyway, it's also hard because he's *very* conservative and from such an insular community. I'm not. My parents never took us to the sun temple when I was young, we didn't really practice Elvish customs at home, but . . . I'm still an elf. There are still things I grew up with that are familiar, food and expectations that don't always line up with the way he thinks things ought to be, and that's what I mean about the little things. Just because I didn't grow up in a conservative household doesn't mean my being an elf shouldn't matter *less,* you know? Plus his family is huge and loud and just . . . it's a lot. They all talk over each other all the time and there are like thirty people in his immediate family! His mom and sisters are all really nice and he claims they love me, but I know they wish he would have settled down with some nice Cornish girl."

Violet had swallowed hard, trying to imagine what it would be like, bringing

Rourke to Christmas dinner with her family in her all-human neighborhood. She could imagine Mrs. Tinsel pressing her face to the glass to get a glimpse of the minotaur, the hooves dinner guest with a *tail*!

"So, you know," Lurielle went on, "it can be a challenge. It's a constant learning curve, and that's for us, which makes the shitty, unsolicited comments from other people even more unwelcome. But," she went on doggedly, "you can't let it matter. There will always be stuff that happens, different priorities and misunderstandings, there will always be people who will say nasty things . . . but it doesn't matter if you work through it together. If you love each other and you're good together, it's worth it. You figure it out." Her bright sapphire eyes had been extra glossy as she looked across the yard to where Khash and Rourke stood over the raised hood of Lurielle's car, a collision of machismo and posturing, threatening to flood the yard with the excess testosterone each man seemed to ooze in the company of the other. "And we're really, really good together. So there's lots of stuff that just doesn't matter."

"Can I ask a question? How-how does he even fit? I mean, he's got to be like seven feet tall and his hands are *huge*, and you're so petite."

Lurielle had hunched, nearly choking on her wine as she laughed, eyes streaming. "This is why I like you, Violet. You're not afraid to ask the important questions. Um, okay actually this is an easy one. Elves are stretchier."

She'd listened with an open mouth as the elf explained her species' diminishing population and the evolutionary changes that had happened as they mated more and more with other species. "They definitely don't teach us that in school though! They want us making Elvish babies with other elves, which is the crux of why most of us are on anxiety medication. Honestly, though, I don't know how some of these human women do it. Like, we'll be out and I'll see a human smaller than you with an orc as big as Khash, and I just want to tell her honey, he's going to perforate your cervix, there is nothing sexy about that."

They had both dissolved into laughter as the men made their way back to the table, and she'd gone back to Rourke's house that night with her heart in her throat, barely waiting for the door to close behind her before she was kissing him. She *did* love him, she was sure of it, and he *was* worth it.

"Is-is this someone from the school, dear?"

"It's not," she answered, dashing her mother's hopes that she was involved in a short-lived post-grad school fling. "He's a bit older than me, very settled, very mature. He's-he's a minotaur. Has his own company and a house here. It's . . . it's a place I can see myself settling, mom. I really want you and Daddy to come visit once I move. You can help me decorate my new place, and-and you can meet him. It would mean a lot to me."

It was going to take her mother time, she knew that. Violet reminded herself, as she hung up the phone, that her own reaction to Cambric Creek and all of its residents, Rourke included, would have been very different ten years earlier, before she'd left her insulated human community. *One disaster down, now on to the next,* she'd thought that morning, readying herself to leave.

Now she shifted, anxiously waiting for destiny to walk through the door. The door jangled open and her head snapped up, but it was only another cluster of university students. She quickly averted her eyes, not needing them to stare her down with the expectation she'd be giving up her small table. She'd already received several hard looks from other patrons: a flinty-eyed goblin toting a laptop and a lovely, haughty woman with light purple skin and long pointed ears, holding the hand of a beautiful little girl, the woman's miniature in a pinafore dress, clutching a stuffed bear.

Violet did her best to ignore the crowd. This was a nice community, she reminded herself, mentally parroting back the gushing things Rourke's neighbor had told her: Cambric Creek was welcoming and inclusive, they valued diversity. "And you're a human!" Lurielle had exclaimed cheerfully. "I hate to admit it, but that's a leg up. Minority hiring makes the company look good." The petite elf had shrugged, giving her an encouraging smile, laughing when Violet's had resembled a grimace.

It's going to be fine. You're going to ace this, it'll be easy, and when it's done you get to have your latte. When she'd entered the coffee shop earlier, Xenna, the barista, had smiled in recognition. "Just the usual?"

"Not yet," replied with a shaky laugh. The fact that she was here often enough to be known by the staff never ceased to thrill her. *See? You belong here. Things are all going to work out.* "I have a job interview . . . um, the ginger tea and a Pep water for now . . . the latte will be my reward when it's done." Now she sat, twisting with nerves as she waited for the arrival of the were cat who would decide her fate. It seemed fitting, she thought, that the interview should be here, in the decadent-smelling coffee shop where so much else had happened.

The bell jangled again and she sipped her water, closing her eyes and inhaling slowly. Rourke had called that morning, just before she'd left her apartment, reminding her that she was overqualified for the position, wishing her luck, and telling her not to worry.

"You're going to be fine," he'd announced with finality, as if it were a forgone conclusion that she'd get the job. "And if they're stupid enough to not love you, then it's their loss. Something else will come up." She wished she had even an ounce of his confidence, his assertiveness, certain that it would help in situations like this . . . but then again, they'd likely not be a very good match if she were just as bossy. "Just don't make yourself upset, okay?" His voice had been gentler then, the soft tone he reserved just for her, and she'd almost been able to feel the tender cradle of his palm around her jaw.

He was right, she told herself steadily. If she didn't get this job, it wouldn't be the end of the world. The knowledge didn't keep her heart from thumping. When she opened her eyes, the sharp smile of the were cat with whom she'd had a video interview the previous week beamed from across the coffee shop. Violet straightened in her seat, returning his smile. It wouldn't be the end of the world, but she badly wanted this job.

Here goes nothing.

Chapter 17

"What is that?!"

Rourke scowled from across the lawn, pushing his messy hair from his eyes long enough to glare before it tumbled back into place. She had previously joked that he didn't own anything less formal than a three-piece suit, and although it was an exaggeration, it was only a slight one. She wasn't sure what shocked her more now—the sight of him casually dressed in the white t-shirt, tight around his biceps and straining across his broad back, or the fact that it was emblazoned with the words MEGA MILKER and the Farm's logo.

"What?" he demanded defensively. "It's not like I wear it out of the house, I'm doing yard work!"

"Yeah, but how did you get it? She held up a hand, groaning, already knowing the answer to her question. "This was in one of the 'reward tiers' I'll bet. How many loads did you need to shoot to work your way up from the coffee cup? Wait, actually, I don't think I want to know."

"Happened a lot faster since you started," he called smugly, restarting the mower with a roar. "I went from the water bottle to the coffee cup in a month. You start milking me like your little cow boys, we might have a tote bag by Halloween, you can use it for trick-or-treating."

He easily dodged the shoe she threw at him and pushed the mower away, the rumble of his laughter competing with the motor.

"Unbelievable," she muttered, shaking her head with a scowl, limping with one sandal into the house. "*I* do all the work, and *you* get the free company swag."

Geillis responded to the text she sent immediately.

How did it go? Do I need to drain one of the neighbors?

She'd had university friends that would have jumped at the chance to have been taken care of by a partner, had had friends who'd done exactly that, trading their independence for the ability to splurge on lunches and shopping and makeup. The thought of having an allowance as an adult had never sat well with her, and she had no doubt Rourke's home would be open to her if she were to express the slightest desire to not find her own place, and even though he'd made good on his promise of spoiling her both in the bedroom and out, wasn't willing to ruin what they had by rushing things. She needed the security blanket of having her own place, her own independence, a way to keep herself from growing too dependent on his money and bossiness and desire to have her around all the time.

I want to talk to someone from your LEASING OFFICE. I don't want you eating your neighbor. Wow, I can't believe I even need to say that. She sighed, smiling before continuing. *I don't want to jinx myself, but I think it went really well. I told them about how my boyfriend took me to Mapplethorpe and that I thought I wouldn't need to rely on so much synthetic reproduction for their project. He seemed really happy with that.* She'd taken all of Rourke's little lessons on who pulled the strings in town and banked on there being a rivalry between families, a hunch that had seemed accurate.

Brilliant. Everything's coming up roses, effluvia. I'll send the number today.

She heard the back door pull open a short while later. The white noise of the mower was gone, and the only sound she could hear coming from outside was the distant yip of Lurielle's little dog, probably barking at a squirrel. She could hear him in the kitchen, shifting around at the back door, pressing his hooves into the silicone gaiters she'd learned most hooves residents wore indoors to prevent catching their sharper edges on carpeting and preserving their bed linens. When she heard the shower in the master bedroom start, she was certain he'd be grateful for some company to soap his back.

She'd never get tired of the sight of him, she was certain. Warm, nutty brown, so strong, and so soft for her when she needed him to be. Water ran in rivulets down his broad back, cutting tracks through his hide as she stepped into the steamy, stall-like shower. He was ticklish just under the base of his tail, and she'd discovered that the seam of his scrotum was covered in the same barely-there velvet as the inside of his soft ears. She kissed his sac, laving her tongue against the spot where he was most sensitive until his cock began to thicken and swell, fat and firm in her hand as the glass shower wall steamed completely.

She loved the way his big balls slapped against her clit when he entered her from behind, just as she loved the way his brow would furrow when he concentrated on his laptop screen; loved the way he snuffled and snorted up her skin before dipping his mouth between her thighs, and the way he sometimes made the same sounds in his sleep, huffing against the pillow as she pressed to his chest. He was solid and warm beneath her when she slept in his bed, and solid and steady for her when her anxiety obliterated her good sense, as steadily as he held her then, aloft in his arms with her legs wrapped around his hips.

She fell apart beneath the water as he pumped upwards into her: squeezing shut her eyes, tightening her legs as her inner walls clenched around him, gripping him tight. He'd slowed his movements then, always enjoying the way she squeezed his cock, before resuming his shallow upwards thrusts. The odd angle meant he was barely halfway in her on every pump, but when his cock erupted inside her, spattering her inner walls with rope after rope of his thick release, Violet kicked, twitching in his arms, the pressure and fullness making her spasm once more.

"How did it go?" His voice was a low whisper into her neck, none of the command; none of the snarl; only the tender softness he reserved for her.

"I think I got it." His arms tightened when her entire body trembled, the act of saying the words aloud so much scarier than merely thinking them in her head, and Violet wondered if he'd be able to tell the difference between her tears and the water still gusting from the shower.

"Good. I knew you would." His cock slipped from her like a particularly corpulent eel, swinging loose with a gush that sent a ripple up her back, splashing to the shower floor like an overturned bucket. "Fuck, it's going to clog the drain . . ." She squealed, tightening her arms around him when he reached, pulling out one of the pods from the net around the shower head and ripping it open, sprinkling the enzyme to the deluge below. After a moment, it began to sizzle, breaking down the protein that would absolutely clog the drain, the protein for which he practically earned a second income. "Everything is going to work out just fine, sweetheart. You'll see."

* * *

"A little higher."

Violet squinted in frustration, not understanding just how high this minotaur wanted her hand to be. It was the third time he'd made the request, and each time she moved her hands farther apart, and each time it evidently wasn't enough.

"Just a little bit more . . ."

"Why don't you tell me exactly where you'd like them," she cut in, tired of playing this guessing game. The bull was close, so close, but something was keeping him from being able to tip over the edge, and the longer they spent playing hotter-colder, the longer it would take him to get there. "I'll do whatever you need me to, it's fine."

"I-I need them to hit my balls."

She closed her eyes, thinking she should have known. She understood exactly what he liked, because she too loved it when her face was pressed to the mattress and her ass high in the air, Rourke's heavy balls slapping into her clit on every thrust. "I can definitely do that." Raising her hand like a paddle, she slapped into the minotaur's sac as he resumed humping against the bench, coming with a groan before long. *I wonder if he's a Mega Milker.*

A pin had come with Rourke's coffee mug, small and white and glinting, and she'd put it on the strap of her bag, wearing it as a badge of honor, wondering if anyone would see it and give her a knowing look. The bull's bottle weighed in at eighteen ounces, not quite the volume of the elite, certainly not tote bag-worthy, she thought, giggling as she loaded the tank on the conveyor belt, her mirth interrupted by an insistent buzzing in her pocket.

By the time she made it into the last collection room of the day, he was already settled against the bench, giving her a lascivious smile as she entered. "I want to be milked like a good little cow today." A command that brokered no argument.

Violet rolled her eyes. "You're completely ridiculous." Thick and veined, fatter than it had the right to be, his cock jerked when she took it up in her slickened palms, and above her, he sighed contentedly.

Their relationship had moved quickly, and she'd fretted to Geillis one afternoon her fear that they would burn out as quickly as they'd ignited, but her friend disagreed.

"It'd be different if you were all passion. I'm not saying there's not passion there," she defended herself, raising a hand to stave off Violet's protestations, "but you actually spend time together. It took him a hundred bloody years to give you the ol' dickory dock, so I don't think you need to worry about flaming out too fast. Besides, luvvie," she added, her voice growing softer, "you lot are here for a minute and then you're gone. Love the ones you love while you got the chance."

She stroked down his cock in a constant tugging motion, pulling on his balls in opposite intervals, smiling when he huffed and snorted above her.

His head was leaking by the time she began to pump his heavy shaft in earnest, his hips meeting the padded bench rhythmically.

"Mmm, don't get any funny ideas," he groaned. "I'm going to be doing this to you later tonight."

"Tonight and tomorrow," she agreed, bringing the tight ring of her fingers over his swollen head. "And Sunday morning."

"Greedy girl." She could tell by the way his breath hitched that he was close to coming, and reached back to retrieve the nozzle.

"And Monday I have to go sign papers for my apartment." Rourke jerked sharply at her words, but she was already working the nozzle down his engorged shaft, grinning at the deep low he let out. The green light clicked on as she milked his heavy balls, feeling the pulse of his eruption thudding through them, as familiar as her own heartbeat. The white-filled bottle was tagged and placed in the corner before she hopped lightly up the short staircase, finding him still laying over the padded bench.

"You got the job?"

"I got the job," she confirmed, leaning in to meet his kiss. "He called just before I came into the room."

"I hope that apartment is a short-term lease."

A riot of butterflies moved through her chest. She loved him, of that she was certain. She couldn't imagine not waking up every weekend to his heavy arm over her, or having dessert first at every meal, and even though it was wildly premature and a conversation she wouldn't dream of broaching until well after her lease was up, she secretly wondered if he'd ever consider having another ring fitted through his wide pink nose.

"It's one year and then month-to-month."

"Perfect," he murmured against her skin, messy pecan hair tickling her cheek. "I wouldn't unpack everything if I were you." His lips were soft and his tongue was hot, and his kiss left her breathless, as it always did, before he pulled himself to his feet to do up his pants.

It was a relief that the new job would be flexible because she'd hate leaving this place, Violet considered. Morning Glory Farm had indeed been a lifeline, in more ways than one. There was no doubt in her mind that if she hadn't clicked that listing, she'd be sitting in the loft above the garage, depressed and anxious and still horribly in debt, with nothing but Carson Tinsley from up the street and her mother's well-meaning suffocation to see her through her days.

No caprine coffee shops, no vampire restaurants, and certainly no Mega Milkerz pin on her bag. She would never have met him, would never know the secret smile he possessed if he'd not been in her life, and she had this place was to thank.

"I have something very important to ask you," he rumbled, arm drawing around her waist, the picture of corporate professionalism once more. "And I'm really hoping you'll say yes."

She turned in his arms, her heart in her mouth. "W-what is it?" His palm was warm as it cupped her face, his thumb gently stroking her cheek, tender and soft and uniquely him. You definitely love him. No question. He checks every box.

"There's something called a chocolate lava explosion at that new arcade restaurant that just opened up, and I need to find out what it is. And I really don't think I'm going to be able to share it. And that place is going to be crawling with kids, so I don't want to go in. So I was thinking, if I order online, maybe you could . . ."

"You want me to go in and get your little kid's dessert that you have no intention of sharing with me?" Her breath hitched when he lifted her, cupping her ass as her legs wrapped around him. *Every. Single. Box.*

"If it's not too much trouble. I'll make it up to you, sweetheart."

She was going to settle into her new life in Cambric Creek, she was going to ace this new job, she was going to listen to his neighbor's very good advice. *If you love each other and you're good together, then it's worth it.*

"You better believe you will."

After all, Violet thought. If a job was worth doing, it was worth doing well.

~ Rourke and Violet may return in other Cambric Creek stories! ~

Welcome to Cambric Creek . . .

Where the neighbors are a little unconventional and the full moon affects more than just the night sky. Sexy werewolves, adorable mothmen, and randy minotaurs welcome you to settle in and make yourself at home! Are you tired of the typical, run-of-the-mill romances featuring the boring Chad next door? Are you longing for a bit of fang and claw in your love story (and maybe a few tentacles for good measure?) Do non-human/human love stories with a scorching heat level get your pulse pumping?

If so, then set a trap for love with Monster Bait

Sweet Berries ~ Coming Soon

The people at the farm—Cal and Brogan and Caleia and the rest—had become a second family, welcoming her into the fold easily. When she'd first applied for the job, she wasn't sure it was going to be enough to put her event planning background to use, but three years later she was busy and happy and wouldn't have it any other way. It was only occasionally, on nights like this when she was lonely and horny, contemplating poor life choices, that she remembered that despite her general happiness, her love life was seriously lacking.

Grace tried to distract herself. As soon as she dropped her bag on the kitchen counter, flicking on the light in her tidy little house, she tried to find some busy work to do—emptying the dishwasher, rinsing the berries, and laying them on a cookie sheet to flash freeze—but the attempted distractions did little to dispel the way she felt itchy in her skin, or the way she pressed her thighs together as she put silverware away, re-exciting the tingle the minotaur's teasing touch had ignited. *Too horny to think.* The swing on her screened-in porch seemed as good a place as any for the tray. The berries, she decided, would keep until morning. The persistent ache between her thighs would not.

The day had been humid and the evening warm, but the light breeze coming in through the open bedroom window was cool, and it was a relief to pull the sundress she'd had on since early that morning over her head. A muffled *whump* sounded in the tree just outside the window as she turned to toss the dress in the hamper, rattling the branches. Whirling in surprise at the noise, Grace waited for a limb to go crashing to the ground, or for the screech of an owl, but several moments passed and nothing came. *Too horny to think, now you're hearing things.*

The soft breeze whispered over her breasts as the lace-edged bra joined the dress in the hamper before she tugged the dampened panties down her hips and kicked them in after. She was able to smell her own arousal, still wet from the big minotaur's teasing. Not going home with him had been a good choice, she knew. She wasn't really interested in him, only the promise of a night of good sex, but co-workers were tricky things, and when push came to shove, she could take care of that on her own. The finger she pressed into her folds came away slick, and as she dragged the moisture across her clit, she couldn't help sighing in pleasure. An answering whicker came from outside the window, freezing her with her hand still between her thighs.

There was something out there.

Instantly her skin prickled at the sensation of eyes resting heavily upon her. Something was there, in the tree, watching her from the darkness. The thought alone of something unknown being just outside her window should have been unsettling, the reality that someone was watching as she undressed was terrifying, should have made her lunge for a towel or her robe, to hide! Instead, her nipples tightened at the thought, a fresh ripple of desire heating her core. *You did say you were going to start being more adventurous . . .* the wet heat of her sex seemed to pulse in agreement against the fingers still pressed there, eliciting another soft moan from her throat. Sure enough, the branches outside rustled as if her voyeur was trying to get a better look.

If they want to watch, you ought to give them a show...

The bed was in the middle of the room, and her mystery watcher had a clear view as she lowered herself to the mattress, sliding to the middle of the bed and opening her legs wide.

* * *

Grace has a job she loves, a community she adores, and plenty of friends . . . but her lack of bedroom action has left this event planner too horny to think. When one ill-advised night at the bar leads to her giving an exhibitionistic show to an unknown presence outside her bedroom window, she thinks she'd hit a new low. When her voyeur turns out to be a nebbishly charming mothman, Grace needs to decide if she can trust her body — and her heart — with this garnet-eyed stranger before he flys out of her life for good.

Sweet Berries is a monster/human romance novella featuring high heat and a lot of heart, with a guaranteed HEA. It is the second book in the Cambric Creek Romance series

About the Author

C.M. Nascosta is an author and professional procrastinator from Cleveland, Ohio. As a child, she thought that living on Lake Erie meant one was eerie by nature, and her corresponding love of all things strange and unusual started young. She's always preferred beasts to boys, the macabre to the milquetoast, the unknown darkness in the shadows to the Chad next door. She lives in a crumbling old Victorian with a scaredy-cat dachshund, where she writes nontraditional romances featuring beastly boys with equal parts heart and heat, and is waiting for the Hallmark Channel to get with the program and start a paranormal lovers series.

Want updates on when new books release? Do you love exclusive shorts? Sign up for my newsletter at: cmnascosta.com and receive an exclusive short in every one. Find me on social media—I love to chat with fans!

You can connect with me on:
- https://cmnascosta.com
- https://twitter.com/cmnascosta
- https://www.facebook.com/authorcmnascosta
- https://www.instagram.com/cmnascosta

Subscribe to my newsletter:
- https://cmnascosta.com

Also by C.M. Nascosta

Girls Weekend

A weekend with friends, fun in the sun, and huge, naked orcs. What could be better?

That's what three suburban elves think when they book a trip to an orc nudist resort, well known for its libidinous residents and hedonistic parties. Ris, Lurielle, and Silva arrive with plans to sample the DTF locals and work on their tans, *not* catch feelings.

When Lurielle meets a syrupy-voiced gentleman who seems interested in more than just a weekend fling, she finds sticking to the plan is easier said than done. From a public bathhouse to a back alley pub, the trip has unintended consequences on the lives of the three work friends and the orcs they meet.

Can a weekend of no-strings sex actually end in love?

CPSIA information can be obtained
at www.ICGtesting.com
Printed in the USA
LVHW081531290821
696392LV00013B/877